*He was sexy as hell and that should have been enough to keep her interested.*

But there was something else about him that seemed to draw her…or call to her. A nebulous thing, right outside her consciousness.

Teal jumped to her feet. "The forensics team will be here soon." She started off toward the abandoned truck—the crime scene—eager to be away from Lucas for a few minutes to gather her wayward thoughts. "I'll go stand by the truck, don't worry about—"

"Teal, stop moving."

The tone of his voice said trouble. But her feet didn't get the message. She couldn't stop the forward motion, but turned her head around to hear what he had to say.

Lucas was racing toward her. "Stop!" he shouted as he reached his arms out for her.

But it was too late. Her foot slipped off the edge of a hidden precipice.

Dear Reader,

A shadow has been creeping across the desert reservation home of the Navajo, and the evil has a name—Skinwalker! Good also has a name in the land between the four sacred mountains—the Brotherhood—a band of young medicine men who have vowed to fight the evil ones in a secret war!

In *Shadow Surrender* I've joined one of my all-time favorite heroes (my editor calls him Lucas Tso-sexy) with an exceptional heroine. I hope you love reading their story as much as I loved writing it! Here are a few Navajo words to help with your understanding:

*Dine*—The Navajo—also known as the People

*Dinetah*—the land between the four sacred mountains where legend says the Dine began (the Four-Corners Big reservation, encompassing parts of Arizona, New Mexico, Colorado and Utah)

*amá sání*—grandmother (maternal)

*anali*—grandmother (paternal)

*bilagáana*—white (as in "white man")

*chindi*—the dark spirits who come with death

*hastiin*—mister, the title for a respected clan elder

*hataalii*—medicine man

*hogan*—the traditional housing of the Navajo, built in an eight-sided design. Now mostly used for religious purposes.

*hozho*—harmony/balance

*jish*—a medicine pouch (usually worn on the belt)

*ya'at'eeh*—hello

*Yei*—the gods of Navajo myths.

Best wishes,

Linda Conrad

# Linda Conrad

# SHADOW SURRENDER

Silhouette®

Romantic
SUSPENSE

 SILHOUETTE BOOKS

ISBN-13: 978-0-373-27527-4
ISBN-10:    0-373-27527-7

SHADOW SURRENDER

Copyright © 2007 by Linda Lucas Sankpill

**Books by Linda Conrad**

Silhouette Romantic Suspense

**Shadow Force #1413
**Shadow Watch #1418
**Shadow Hunter #1450
**Shadow Surrender #1457

Silhouette Desire

The Cowboy's Baby Surprise #1446
Desperado Dad #1458
Secrets, Lies...and Passion #1470
*The Gentrys: Cinco #1508
*The Gentrys: Abby #1516
*The Gentrys: Cal #1524
Slow Dancing With a Texan #1577
The Laws of Passion #1609
Between Strangers #1619
†Seduction by the Book #1673
†Reflected Pleasures #1679
†A Scandalous Melody #1684

*The Gentrys
†The Gypsy Inheritance
**Night Guardians

## LINDA CONRAD

was inspired by her mother, who gave her a deep love of storytelling. "Mom told me I was the best liar she ever knew. And that's saying something for a woman with an Irish-storyteller's background," she says. Linda has been writing contemporary romances for Silhouette Books for six years. Besides telling stories, her passions are her husband and family, and finding the time to read cozy mysteries and emotional love stories. Linda keeps busy and is happy living in the sunshine near the Florida Keys. Visit Linda's Web site at www.lindaconrad.com.

To Maureen Emmons, with all my thanks for her wonderful title suggestion. And thanks to everyone else who sent in terrific "SHADOW" ideas! There were some great titles there, and your efforts are truly appreciated!

# *Chapter 1*

The Four-Corners reservation hung suspended in the bluish-lavender twilight that only comes to high desert in early fall. Winds blew down canyons and across bloodred spires of sandstone, spreading the scents of sage, cedar and the pungent odors of smoke and musk.

Special Agent Teal Benaly's nose itched as something light and gossamer blew past her face. She never allowed herself to be struck by flights of fancy, most things were easier to deal with in terms of black or white. But when a feather's shades of sand and desert gray had caught her eye, even in the low light of dusk, it seemed like a kind of message. She dropped one hand from the shale-rock ledge and bent to pick it up.

Drawing the softness of feathers across her cheek while she stared off into space, Teal let herself forget for the moment the potential dangers of Many Caves Canyon. Instead of thinking about business, her thoughts turned to birds. She'd both heard them calling and seen a few in flight earlier. But why had this particular feather got caught on the breeze and managed to glide by her nose right then? It seemed a strange thing to happen in the stillness of twilight.

There were so many things about her birth home in Navajoland that currently confused and confounded her. Of course, even as a child she hadn't known a damn thing about birds. She'd grown up a *city* Navajo.

The fingers of her left hand were still gripping the ledge to keep herself from sliding down the one-hundred-foot drop-off. However, she imagined it might be smart to start paying greater attention to her surroundings. Teal stuffed the feather into the back pocket of her heavy khaki pants then grabbed for the granite outcropping with her free hand and held tight with both hands. It was clear, even to a city Navajo, how easy it might be to fall down this steep path and break her neck.

But there was a job to do here. So she kept moving.

The call to check out an abandoned truck at the bottom of a ravine had come too late in the afternoon for her to arrive before sunset. She had no idea why a tribal police officer hadn't been sent to check it out instead of the newest FBI special agent.

Damn her superiors in Washington, anyway. They knew the last station she'd wanted to be assigned to right out of training at Quantico was the Navajo reservation. Just because she spoke the language—a little.

And looked like she belonged here—sort of. It was still not fair to post her to a field office in the one place in the entire world that she hated most.

Taking a breath, she reminded herself she'd been brought here to the reservation at the Navajo Nation's request. The Bureau had sent her in to work on a special joint tribal and FBI operation.

It had been an honor to be given such an important assignment right out of training. But she couldn't imagine that an old abandoned truck would have anything to do with her job.

Nevertheless. She had been sent to check out the truck, and check it out she would. Thank goodness a three-quarter moon would soon be helping to light her way.

As she stood in the growing shadows, straightening her jacket and checking her holstered weapon, something brushed her cheek. *Holy hell.* Looking around, she saw nothing in the deepening dusk.

It happened again. Cripes. She let out a shriek and reached for her Glock, but never managed to get the weapon out of its holster.

All of a sudden, small dark flying *things* were zipping past her from all sides. Oh. My. God.

*Bats*.

Swiping wildly at the air around her head, trying to keep them away from her face, Teal took both hands off the ledge. And immediately regretted the move.

The rocks under her feet began to slide—a little bit at first. Then the good rubber soles of her shoes refused to catch hold against the sharp granite surfaces, even as she was trying desperately to keep her balance.

In the end, she landed hard on her butt and began a free-fall slide downhill that would've scared her to death—if she'd had a moment to actually think about it.

Wasn't this the time when her whole life was supposed to flash in front of her eyes? Except—right now her eyes were squeezed shut and she was screaming loud enough to keep the images...the fear...and the *bats*...far, far away.

Lucas Tso heard the woman screaming and looked around. Where was she? Close. But where?

He wasn't surprised at the high-pitched call for help. After all, that was why he was out here in Many Caves Canyon after sunset.

The Bird People had given him a warning. And he had come, because for days he'd been dreaming about saving a woman. A dark-haired and dark-eyed woman whose face was never clear in his dreams. He'd had many dreams over his lifetime. But never before had the circumstance seemed so urgent or had the person been so unfocused.

Above him—that's where the screams were coming from. If he climbed the shale path fast enough, he should make it in time to intercept her fall.

He moved quickly past red sandstone boulders and around granite obstacles. The shale was slick and slippery, but he dug his moccasins deep into the rocks and pumped his legs to climb even faster.

Who was she? Could she have anything to do with the secret Skinwalker war that had been going on in Dinetah over the last few years?

Was she one of *them?* Or one of their victims?

The Bird People were allies of the Brotherhood in this war. Lucas knew they would never deliberately lead him into a trap. But this was so different from a normal attack.

Time enough later to ponder the significance of the dreams and of the woman. For now he had to first find her, then figure out how to save her.

Looking upward through the moonlight, he spotted a flash of light-colored clothing as it careened down the path toward him. A few more yards and he would be in position to stop her fall.

He steeled himself for the jolt, and began chanting a medicine man prayer that he would make it there before her body rolled in the wrong direction and headed right over the edge of the cliff.

Teal was trying in vain to stop her fall. She jammed her heels into the path but only succeeded in rolling herself over and totally losing control.

She raised her arms in front of her face to shield her eyes from the pointy rocks. If she had been religious, this would have been a good time to pray, but she had no idea how.

Her clothes were already being ripped by the knife-sharp rocks, and her face and hands were bruised and bleeding. What would happen to the rest of her skin if her clothes completely shredded and fell away before the fall came to a stop?

This downward tumble had to end. Now. Teal braced herself to put one last desperate effort into stopping.

Then, miraculously, it was over. But how?

"Can you stand? Is anything broken?"

Who said that? Uh-oh.

Scrambling to her feet, she was suddenly much less worried about broken bones and bleeding skin than she was about facing a deep-voiced stranger in the shadows of this canyon wilderness. Damn.

But when she finally found herself upright, her head was swimming and she reached out blindly to steady herself. Strong arms loomed out from the darkness to give her support.

Still slightly scared, over both her brush with death and the spooky guy who'd come to her rescue, she nonetheless felt relieved to be alive and apparently safe. Teal began taking long breaths and fought for control. At the same time, she reviewed her physical state. Nothing seemed to be broken. But everything hurt.

"You will be sore for quite a while, I'm afraid," said the deep-voiced shadow beside her as if he'd read her thoughts. "But if nothing's broken, I think I may be able to help with the cuts and scrapes. Will you let me try?"

"What?" She eased away and peered at his face. "Who the hell are you? And why did you happen to be out here at the right place at the exact right moment?"

For a few seconds there was dead silence. It was enough time for a first-in-her-class sharpshooter to draw her weapon from its holster under her ripped jacket.

"Don't move," she demanded as she pointed the Glock in his direction. "And answer my question."

The outline of the man stilled. "My name is Lucas Tso. I am of the Big Medicine People, born for the Bitter Water Clan. I'm a native artisan, specializing in Navajo designs…and a medicine man who can help you with your injuries. I have no weapons and no bad intentions. There is no need for the gun."

"Don't make any sudden moves," she warned. "I'm FBI Special Agent Teal Benaly. I'll show you my ID— right after I check out your story."

"You intend to frisk me, Special Agent?" he asked, reading her mind again.

She could hear the smile in his voice and it added to her irritation. "Turn around, hands against the ledge and spread your legs."

"Yes, ma'am. But I must warn you to be careful on the rocks. They're very slippery."

"Yeah, I got that, thanks."

He turned around. After temporarily sliding her weapon into the waistband of her slacks, she moved one leg between his two to stop him from running, exactly as she had been taught. This would be her first chance to do in real life what they'd practiced.

The man was taller than she was. She guessed he was six-two to her five-eight. But she could trip him up if she kept her leg positioned just right.

That was the method she'd learned. But her training

had not included the frisson of electricity that jolted through her the minute she touched the guy.

Jeez. What the hell was that all about?

Biting down on the inside of her cheek to keep from actually moaning aloud at the unusual and pleasurable warmth she'd felt emanating from his body, Teal went to work. She checked his jacket pockets and came up empty.

The weird sensations rocketing around in her body were totally out of line, and seemed rather ridiculous considering only a minute ago she'd been so frightened. Maybe her brain and gut had scrambled in the fall.

She reached under his jacket and began patting him down. Oh, God. Her breath hitched in her throat.

Keep your head, girl. This guy could be anybody.

Right side first. Keeping a tight grip on her emotions and a keen eye on his every move, she ran a hand down his body and checked his ankle for hidden weapons. Nothing.

Nothing—except the firm feel of toned thigh and calf muscles under his jeans. Crap.

She patted up the inside of the right leg, hesitated for less than a second, then moved down the inside of his left leg. This one time, if there were weapons hidden in his crotch, she would have to die for lack of checking.

Coming up the outside of his left leg, she found a wallet in his back pocket and a leather pouch attached to his belt. Taking a deep breath, she was miserable to discover his possessions smelled of musk and sweat and virile man. She had to shake her head slightly to clear it. Without giving him warning, she reached around him and undid his belt buckle, sliding both belt and pouch off him in one fast move.

Nice execution, Special Agent, she congratulated herself. She'd done a good job on both the lightning moves and on getting through the pat-down without collapsing in a quivering heap at his feet.

"What's in the bag?" she asked and stepped back.

"Medicine-man supplies. No weapons."

A load of bull? "Turn around—slowly." She pulled her Glock from its resting place and stuffed his wallet and bag into her jacket pockets.

"*Every* movement needs to be slow on this shale," he told her as he shifted to face her in the darkness.

"Right. Well, *carefully* walk the path in front of me, please. No jerking or twisting. We're going to move down to the canyon floor near that abandoned vehicle so I can check the wallet and bag for myself."

"Abandoned vehicle?"

Did he really not know about the truck? "I'll ask the questions for now. Start walking."

As they went, he kept his hands high where she could see his movements, and didn't seem to have any trouble at all balancing himself on the jagged rock. But she was forced to hang on to the granite shelf with one hand and keep her weapon at the ready with the other.

Within minutes, both her hands were stinging like crazy. She could feel a trickle of warm liquid, probably blood, rolling down her cheek. Still, she was alive and vowed to continue her vigilance in order to stay that way.

But her mind was reeling with what had been happening. What was with this guy? He kept saying things that made her think he had been reading her mind. There were just too many strange coincidences tonight.

At last they made it to the canyon floor. Down on level ground, they were stepping on packed sand rather than slippery rocks.

"This is the headwater of the Kayenta Caves dry wash," Lucas told her. "During heavy storms, the underground aquifer that supplies the Kayenta mine area overflows and runs out of the cliffs into this arroyo. That's why you're walking across packed sand now instead of rocks and pebbles."

Damn it. He was doing it again. It was creepy.

When they had walked within thirty feet of the abandoned truck and could see its outline in the moonlight, she came to a halt. "Hold on. Before we get any closer, I'd like to go over your ID and get a few more answers."

"All right," he said and turned to face her.

The moon was high in the sky now and most of his features were visible. He had a longish, narrow face and a lean, narrow body—all shoulders and not much hip. Exactly the way she remembered her father's physique. Must be that was a common male Navajo trait. Something she would be wise to remember for her assignment.

Lucas's dark hair was also on the long side. Down past

the collar of his jacket, it gave him a slightly sexy but comfortable appearance. Teal felt herself starting to relax.

From what she could make out of his face in the shadows, he had a beautiful high forehead, spectacular sharp angles of jaw and cheekbone, and a broad nose to keep the whole thing from being perfect. Though she was unable to tell the color of his eyes at the moment, she knew they were studying her.

She pulled the flashlight from its spot at her waist in order to study his wallet and flicked the light switch. But nothing happened.

"It might've broken as you fell," Lucas said drily.

"Maybe." She put the flashlight back in place, stuffed the wallet in her pocket again and tightened her grip on the semiautomatic. "You never answered my question about what you were doing up on that path at this time of night. It was a bit too handy that you were right there to save me."

"I… Have you ever heard anything about a group of medicine men calling themselves the Brotherhood?"

"No. Should I have?"

"I thought you might've. We're a legitimate society banded together to fight neighborhood crime in Dinetah. Sort of a citizens' watch committee."

"Okay. Let's say I buy that. What neighborhood are you watching way out in such a desolate canyon?"

"We got a tip that something bad was going down here tonight." He shifted his feet and Teal wished to hell she could see his eyes. "Look," he began again. "Do you know an agent by the name of Kody Long?

He works on various projects for the FBI on the reservation."

"Yes," she replied. "I've met Special Agent Long and have even worked with him a time or two. Why?"

"He'll vouch for me. He's my cousin and knows all about the Brotherhood."

Not sure her cell phone would work at the bottom of a canyon, Teal dug in her inside jacket pocket and pulled it out to check the signal. She got lucky for once tonight.

"The signal is weak, but I can put in a call for Special Agent Long. We'll wait until I can verify your story."

"I could reach him faster."

"Oh?"

"The Brotherhood has a specially-connected family satellite phone system. I can dial him direct."

"Where's your phone? I patted you down and didn't find one. Is it back up on the trail?"

"Front pocket of my jeans. You missed it."

Figured. She was doing everything wrong tonight. Next she would probably have to take the damn phone from him, too.

But not if she could help it. "Take off your jacket. Nice and slow, please. And then drop it on that flat rock beside you."

He did as she asked. She could see his torso much better in the moonlight. Without thinking, she sighed. But the soft whooshing sound suddenly seemed terribly frivolous coming from her own mouth. She choked at her own stupidity.

"Okay," she muttered through a cough. She was trying desperately to clear her throat and her head. "Now, keep your right hand high above your head and very carefully take the phone from your pocket with the other hand."

"Did you already spot the fact I'm right-handed?" he asked with a smile. "Or was that a calculated guess?"

"Just do as I say. And once again…with nice slow movements."

She watched him remove a thin, black case that was probably a phone. But for all she knew, the person standing in front of her could be one of the terrorists who were supposedly infiltrating the U.S. through the remote areas of the rez.

She'd been warned to watch out for them. And that case he was holding might actually explode when he opened it.

"I'm not suicidal, Special Agent Benaly. You have nothing to fear."

Shoot. There he went again, answering questions she hadn't even asked.

Before she could react, he flicked his wrist and the phone opened up. He held it high where she could get a good look at the lighted faceplate.

"Fine," she said and shook her head with chagrin. She was still moving a step behind this guy. "Dial the number and then hand it to me."

He punched a button and handed it over.

Keeping her weapon trained directly at his gut, she gingerly took the phone from his hand. By the time she put the receiver to her ear, she could hear a deep male voice on the other end.

The voice identified itself as Special Agent Long, then asked if it was an emergency and if Lucas Tso was all right. She held off the questions until she could verify the voice's identity. First she asked him a question about one of the times they had met here on the reservation, and then asked about what was served at a cafeteria back at Quantico—an answer that only another special agent would know.

He passed her tests.

"This is not an emergency and Lucas Tso appears to be well," she finally answered. "We are standing in one of the ravines at Many Caves…"

"Yes, I know where you are. I have you on GPS. Do you need help?"

Special Agent Kody Long's continued insistence that something must be wrong threw her off. It sent a chill down her spine and made her wonder what she'd missed.

"May I talk to Agent Long?" At the sound of Lucas's warm, bass voice, she looked up to find he'd moved in close.

Too close. But he was deliberately standing in a nonthreatening manner with his hand held toward her, palm out.

Since she couldn't find her voice at the moment, Teal simply nodded and handed back the phone. Her shoulders slumped and the arm holding the Glock relaxed. Having her weapon pointed at the ground was against all procedure, though, so she reholstered it.

Then she stood quite still and listened to one side of the conversation between cousins.

"No, no sign of…trouble," Lucas said into the phone. "I'm not sure. She says she's here to check out an abandoned truck."

Well, he didn't seem to mind that she knew they were talking about her. That at least made him appear honest.

"Yeah, we could use your help. Bring a light, Cousin. In fact, a lot of lights would come in handy if we're going to be able to check out that truck tonight."

*We?* There was no way she would let a layperson assist in any investigation of hers. She would have to find a way to tell Lucas thanks for saving her life, but bah-bye now.

He closed the phone and stuck it back in his pocket. "Ten to fifteen minutes tops. Kody will be bringing lights. While we wait, let me tend to your injuries. That cut under your eye might need a stitch."

Huh? "How is your cousin Kody going to get here that fast?"

She heard Lucas chuckle, though she couldn't see his expression in the shadows.

"My cousin was right up the road. And where we're standing is only ten minutes from the highway."

"Ten minutes? What are you talking about? You and I walked down that shale path for nearly a half hour. And I had been climbing down it for fifteen minutes before you stopped my fall. How is that ten minutes from the highway?"

"Didn't you stop to consider how a truck would've

gotten itself down into the bottom of a ravine?" he asked with a small snicker. "Someone drove it in and left it parked there." Without waiting for her, he'd answered his own question.

When she simply stood there open-mouthed, he continued, "They had to come down the gravel road from the highway. It turns to packed sand about a half mile up the dry streambed from here. But it's doable by four-wheel drive."

"There's a road?" Son-of-a...

"Ah, Special Agent love, looks like you might need a lesson or two in getting around Dinetah. Let's talk about that and our friendship while we wait for my cousin."

Oh, Lord. The two of them were certainly never going to stay close enough to be friends. Nuh-uh. Impossible.

"We'll talk about it," he whispered, once again echoing her thoughts. "For now, come sit by me on this rock so I can clean your wounds."

"No... Yes." She was sputtering. "But... But..."

## Chapter 2

Lucas carefully dabbed water from his pouch onto the back of her hands. He was stunned when she relented and was willing to let him touch her. Teal must be in much more pain than she was letting on. Trying to clean the dust from her cheeks and chin, he worked as gently as possible.

He heard the soft intake of breath that telegraphed her true state, but she never flinched while he rubbed salve over her wounds. Though she was frightened and hurting, Teal Benaly was being very brave.

Back on the shale path, when a shaft of moonlight had suddenly lit up her face, he'd been staggered. He was seldom surprised by anything anymore. But not only was she the dark, *faceless* woman he had recently dreamed of saving, she was also the sexy Navajo woman with the wide chocolate eyes and full lips that he had been seeing in his dreams off and on for…years.

It should tell him something that he had never even considered that the two women could be the same person, but his mind had been focused on the Skinwalkers lately. So many hurt innocents. So many deaths.

But now, how was he going to manage to act as if the two of them were complete strangers? How would that be possible when he *knew* the softness on the backs of her knees and when he could have described the feel and the scent of her thick ebony hair without ever coming anywhere near her in real life?

"That doesn't look much like a medicine-man cure," she said, pulling him back from the dream. He was inching toward her with a butterfly bandage in his hand.

"It's a cure *this* medicine man uses," he said quietly. "I think it might work well enough to close that gash under your eye without a suture."

He had to keep acting as though nothing was different. As though his whole world hadn't stopped spinning and gone completely out of balance.

When the bandage was finally in place, she released a pent-up breath. Lucas knew she had to be aching all over, yet she sat beside him with her shoulders back and her chin raised high.

He wished to hell he could wrap her up in a cotton cocoon and suspend her from a star while her body healed itself. There was nothing he would be able to do or say, in any language, to make her pain completely disappear.

"I have a special natural medicine with me that could make that aching kneecap of yours more tolerable," he told her. "Will you take it?"

"No," she said through gritted teeth. "And stop that."

"Stop what?"

"Stop saying things that make it seem like you can hear what I'm thinking. It's creeping me out."

"Sorry." But he wasn't. He was plenty creeped out himself by finding the woman he had been dreaming about since they had both been children. Having her feel nervous, too, seemed only fair.

He'd always been positive that he would live to a ripe old age and never get the chance to meet the woman he had come to crave in his dreams. Yet here she was—sitting beside him in the moonlight.

"You haven't been in Dinetah very long, have you?"

When she reared back and narrowed her eyes at him, he suppressed a grin.

"That was a guess," he said with a quiet chuckle. "But if it weren't true, you would never have been climbing down that path after dark. Most of the local people know it's dangerous to be in remote areas of the reservation at night."

"Dangerous how? I've been here six months and I haven't noticed anything too dangerous—day or night."

When he only smiled at her, she began to stutter.

"Well…I mean, besides falling on the rocks and nearly rolling off the side of a cliff."

He wasn't about to tell her the truth of the dangers in the night for the lands of Dinetah. She would never believe him anyway. Not yet.

Instead of answering her question, he asked one of his own. "Did something frighten you up there on the path? You look like a smart woman. Why'd you let go of the ledge?"

She blinked. And the expression on her face was definitely embarrassment. It was the first time she had shown any real emotion except for fear. Lucas was praying she hadn't had a run-in with any of the Skinwalkers. How would he explain…

"It was the bats." She shrugged a shoulder and turned her face.

"Bats? What about them?" He had never heard of any Skinwalker witchery that could turn humans into bats. But then, anything was possible these days in Dinetah.

"They just appeared. Right out of a crack in the rocks. And they flew all around my head, and they were…"

"Did any of them strike you? Bite you?"

She shook her head. "No, but…"

Relieved, he touched her shoulder. "Bats aren't anything to be afraid of. Bats are mammals, but like the Bird People, they're part of our world. Bats sleep in caves during the day and go looking for food at dusk. They weren't trying to hurt you, just heading off for breakfast."

"Do you want to explain the 'Bird People' comment?"

Lucas did not intend to answer her question directly. So he tried to deflect her interest with another question of his own.

"Who are your people, Teal?"

"I grew up in Denver, but my parents were both Navajo."

"Since you are quite obviously Dineh, and Benaly is a common Navajo name, I already assumed you're a *city* Navajo. But didn't your mother ever teach you about your lineage? Who are your clan ancestors?"

"Oh. You mean like you said you were born of something for somebody? No, my mother isn't into reservation stuff, she didn't grow up here. But before he died, my father did try to teach me some of those kinds of things. And my great-aunt, his mother's sister, used to tell me stories about the Navajo when we came to visit her during summer vacations."

"Your father died? I'm sorry for your loss." He'd felt the punch of her grief the minute she'd uttered the words—even though her voice had remained steady and her face showed no emotion.

"Thanks, but it happened when I was eleven. That's a long time ago now."

"Uh-huh," he mumbled under his breath. But he knew that her spirit still felt the pain as if it had happened yesterday.

"What does knowing the names of my clan have to do with 'Bird People' anyway?" she asked, apparently trying to drag the conversation back her way.

"Everyone and everything that is native to Navajoland belongs to a clan. It's how we identify ourselves and know our place in the world." Of course, his place in the Navajo world had always been rather tentative. Not because of his clan, but because of who and what he was.

But he was not the subject of their conversation.

When she looked up at him with confusion in her eyes, he continued. "The birds belong to their own clans. They are *of* the Bird People. Some are *for* the red-shouldered hawk clan, others *for* the raven clan—and so on. But they all know where they come from and where they belong."

Well, most of them did, he thought grimly. But he refused to mention the unnatural and out-of-balance Navajo medicine men who had learned to turn themselves into animals and birds in order to wreak havoc for greed and power. No, the doomed Skinwalker Raven and his buddies like the freak vultures would not be a great topic of conversation to have with this beautiful *city* Navajo.

At least, not tonight.

"*Ya'at'eeh.*" Kody Long's voice came out of the darkness, surprising Lucas. Why hadn't he heard his cousin's thoughts as the FBI agent approached? Things seemed suddenly to be slipping totally out of his control.

Teal felt Lucas's body tense beside her as the surprising voice came out of the darkness. She automatically reached for her weapon. But before she got there, Lucas stayed her hand and shook his head.

"It is Kody Long with the lights," he told her softly.

*"Ya'at'eeh,"* he called out as an answer. "We're over here, Cousin."

In seconds, a flashlight beam appeared out of the darkness and headed toward them. The two males greeted each other with Navajo grunts and pointed looks. A strange expression passed between them, without the uttering of any spoken words to give away its meaning. It struck Teal as slightly odd, but this Lucas character was already *way* strange in her opinion.

Kody directed the beam of light at Lucas, somehow satisfying himself in a moment or two that her savior was truly okay. But as the light from the flashlight illuminated Lucas's face, she got her first good look at his eyes—and found herself trying to catch her breath.

The man was riveting, his eyes magnetic. If he was this spectacular now, what would he be like in broad daylight? Whew. She needed to regain her focus.

Then Kody turned the light toward her. "Hell. Look at you. What the devil happened?"

She straightened her shoulders and damned near saluted the other Special Agent. "I took a small tumble down the shale path, that's all. But nothing's broken. I'm a little dirty but perfectly fine."

Lucas cleared his throat. "Well, perhaps *fine* may be a slight exaggeration. Special Agent Benaly is cut and badly bruised, but she's doing a great job of keeping her professional composure. Very impressive."

Biting her tongue to stay silent instead of telling her

savior to keep his opinions to himself turned out to be extremely difficult for Teal. But she knew Kody would not appreciate her telling his cousin off. It would sound rude. Especially since the man had, in fact, saved her life.

It hit her finally that not only was it rude, saying such a thing was definitely crass, and not at all like something she would do. What in the world had come over her? She was a professional and a fully-fledged Special Agent. A clumsy fall shouldn't be messing with her mind this way.

She stiffened her spine and stood up on shaky legs. "I appreciate you bringing lights, but…" The ground below her started to roll and she was forced to sit back down on the rock next to Lucas. "Oh."

Both men turned concerned gazes in her direction.

"You all right?" Kody asked. "Maybe we should take you to the hospital."

Lucas stood and faced his cousin. "She'll be okay in a few minutes. She wants to stay and finish her assignment. She would also like a moment to talk to you alone. Give me the keys. I'll go get the lights from your pickup."

Kody dug in his pants pocket and threw Lucas the keys. Then he sat down next to Teal.

"No kidding, you look pale and beat-up," Kody said when Lucas had moved away into the darkness. "Are you sure we shouldn't get you to a doctor?"

She was so angry over Lucas making all those assumptions about her that she could barely speak. "Is he really your cousin?" she asked through gritted teeth.

"Certainly. And he's also a good friend. He saved your life, right?"

"Yes. But…forgive me, but doesn't he seem a little weird to you?"

"Weird?" Kody seemed to mull that over for a minute. "Yeah, I guess I know what you're talking about. Lucas is…well…we call him a 'sensitive.' He's different in that respect from the rest of us. But we all can be a little weird some of the time."

"A sensitive? You mean he *sees* things before they happen?" She waved her arms around like a bird. "Like, whoo whoo whoo, things that go bump in the night?"

Kody shot her a narrowed-lip frown. "If I were you, Teal, I would be very careful of making fun of things on the reservation that you don't understand. You've been assigned to Dinetah to do a job. And in order to get that job done, you'll need both to learn the lay of the land and get a better sense of the people on it.

"If you intend to be closed-minded," he continued. "Perhaps being transferred elsewhere would be more appropriate."

Teal knew what being transferred out before her job was complete would mean to her fledgling career. Demotion.

"No, no," she stuttered. "I wasn't being disrespectful. I am truly grateful that Lucas saved my life. It's only that he…makes me uncomfortable."

"Unfortunately, he's been doing that same thing to people most of his life. Try to see things through his eyes. It must be a great burden to know what's going to happen before it happens, and to know for certain when people are lying or telling the truth. I know I wouldn't want to have that gift—most of the time."

Ah, hell. Now she was feeling guilty about the angry thoughts she'd been having about the guy. Sheesh.

"Okay, I'm sorry. It's just that…" She let her words trail off because she didn't know how to explain herself. Being around Lucas was driving her a tiny bit insane.

She could only hope that he would leave soon. Then she could go back to work and stop wondering about him and the strange and intense sensations he was causing.

"I can tell you that Lucas is a good guy to have around," Kody added. "He's a world-renowned artisan. And luckily for you, he is also a world-class athlete. He…"

A beam of light interrupted him as it scanned their bodies. Lucas came back into the small clearing where she and Kody were sitting on the rock. He was carrying flashlights and lanterns.

"I think six or seven lights ought to be enough. We can triangulate them just right in order to get a look at that abandoned truck," Lucas said. "As we check it out, you'll have to tell me what you hope to find."

He wasn't leaving yet? Why not?

For some reason, she'd assumed that when Kody arrived, Lucas would feel free to leave. Maybe he thought she needed him to stay and take care of her until the dizzying effects of the fall wore off. Well, she didn't.

And she intended to prove it to him. "Thanks, Lucas. I'll take the lights from here." She stood up as carefully as possible without letting either man see how shaky she felt.

Standing beside her, Lucas stilled and studied her in the flashlight beam for a minute. Then he turned over the flashlights and lanterns—one at a time.

"I did some routine scouting around the truck area on the way back from Kody's pickup," he said quietly. "Nothing's stirring. If you'd like the opportunity to check out the truck alone, I could stay here and talk about Brotherhood business with Kody for a few minutes."

Teal nearly fell at his feet with relief. He really did seem to know what she wanted without her having to say a word.

"Thanks." It would take her a good long while to come to terms with what she thought of this man. At which point she would surely find a way to thank him properly for saving her life. In the meantime, she needed space.

She turned to address the other Special Agent. "Do you mind letting me do my job alone this time, Kody? I'd like to prove I'm capable of handling an assignment without everything dissolving into a disaster. I really don't need to be saved every five minutes."

"Sure," Kody answered. "Take your time. I'll be hanging around to drive you back to your car when you're finished."

Lucas watched her disappear into the black of night, heading off through the sand and yellow snakeweed toward the abandoned truck. She would be okay by herself. There didn't seem to be any Skinwalker activity in the area. And he would be within shouting distance if she needed him.

"So what's really going on, Cuz?" Kody asked. "Was this a Skinwalker attack or what?"

Lucas turned so he could talk to Kody quietly. "Not that I can tell. The Bird People let me know a woman was going to be in trouble. They thought the way she was coming down that shale was obviously all wrong.

"But she says bats scared her and she fell," he continued. "Doesn't seem too unnatural."

"No, just klutzy." Kody was chuckling softly to himself.

Lucas didn't care for the image his cousin's words painted. In his opinion, Teal Benaly was lithe and graceful. But he decided against making a big deal of it. He still wasn't sure why he had been dreaming of her and where their relationship would go.

"I haven't felt any Skinwalker activity in the area since we've been here," he said instead. "I did hear a distant burrowing owl calling a while back. And I can't figure out where the Bird People have gone. It seems too quiet."

"Too quiet is good." Kody shook his head. "Ever since the last skirmish that nearly took my brother's life, it's been easier to think. When it's quiet, everything seems almost normal."

"I haven't seen Hunter in weeks," Lucas remarked as he thought of the last time he'd seen Kody's brother.

"He's on temporary leave from the Tribal Police so he can work with Michael Ayze. They've taken up the Brotherhood's quest to find that map to the ancient parchments—before the Skinwalkers have a chance to steal it back."

The map had almost been in the Brotherhood's hands once. Now, even they didn't have a clue where it was. It had been stolen and buried by a Skinwalker traitor. The one who had died for his trouble.

Lucas knew the Brotherhood felt their best hope to rid Dinetah of the scourge of the Skinwalkers would come in the form of those parchments. And having a human bloodhound like Kody's brother, Hunter Long, helping Michael Ayze locate the map should make their odds even better.

The Brotherhood was desperate to find a way of slowing down the evil shadow that had been spreading across the reservation for the last few years. They all prayed the map would be the key to unlocking the answers for restoring balance.

Thoughts of harmony and balance brought Lucas right back to thinking of his dream woman. "Why is Teal really here in Many Caves Canyon tonight?" Lucas asked his cousin. "What does the FBI care about an old abandoned truck?"

"I did some checking after you called me. I'd thought it was interesting that the Bureau would assign another Navajo agent to the Navajo reservation without a good covert reason. It's too…expected."

Kody smiled into the darkness. "*I'm* only out here because I can speak the language and know the area. They needed me to help halt the terrorist threat coming in from Mexico. *And* I asked to be assigned here."

Lucas nodded. He knew Kody had deliberately come home a couple of years ago so he could become a secret warrior for the Brotherhood. It was a good thing, too. Kody had done many heroic deeds so far during their war—including saving his new *bilagaana* wife's life.

"Anyway," Kody went on. "A buddy told me Teal is here to work on a joint FBI and Navajo nonpublic project. Apparently, the Navajo Tribal Council has quietly asked the feds for help in stopping the arson and so-called accidents that've been occurring around the Black Mesa mining area.

"She's not exactly undercover," he amended. "Only supposed to nose around to see what one Navajo can find out."

Lucas nodded again. He knew all about the problems the Navajo nation had been having with the coal mines that supplied the Mohave Generating Plant. He himself was ambivalent about letting a white man's coal company rip Dineh treasure right out of the earth, destroying precious groundwater in the process.

He admitted the coal mines had brought jobs that were desperately needed. But at what price?

"But Teal doesn't know..." Lucas hesitated, not sure what he could say about the sincere and intense young woman agent. "Well, she doesn't know a lot about Dinetah, and doesn't have a good grasp of the language. How is she supposed to find out anything?"

"That sort of fact doesn't usually hold much sway in Washington. They think because she looks like a redskin...and she was born on the rez—send her."

"Hmm. She could get herself in a world of trouble wandering around out here alone."

Kody nodded sadly. "Yeah, but..."

Suddenly, Lucas's senses picked up. Teal was already in trouble. He jumped, turning to head in her direction—as a light came rushing toward them out of the dark.

"Omigosh," she said, out of breath, when she appeared behind the flashlight beam. "You've got to come."

"What's up?" Kody asked warily, as he stood.

"It's...it's..." She put her hands on her knees and gulped for breath.

Lucas fully expected to hear that something evil had attacked her. Or at least that she'd seen a strange wild animal or bird that had scared her again. He prepared himself to begin chanting the sacred words that could ward off a Skinwalker attack.

"In that truck," she finally blurted out.

Kody took her by the shoulders. "What is it? What did you see?"

"A guy's dead in there." Now that Lucas could study her, she seemed more enthusiastic than frightened.

"Really," she gasped. "I checked. He's definitely dead."

## Chapter 3

Could this night possibly get any worse? From the very moment she'd fallen on the shale path, everything had gone downhill.

Pun deliberately intended, Teal chided herself. What a doofus she'd been. First she had to be rescued from a potentially fatal fall. Then she'd found the dead body—and immediately begun acting like the rookie she was. Ah, hell.

It wasn't like she had never seen a corpse before. She had. A couple of times. But the shock of it had reminded her too much of a similar trauma from a long time ago. One she was constantly trying to keep out of her conscious mind.

Good thing Kody had made finding a body sound

like an ordinary occurrence. His professional demeanor had quieted her anxiety in a hurry.

"How do you know the guy's dead and not sleeping one off?" Kody asked as he and Lucas accompanied her back through the brush and sand to the old panel truck.

She had to find at least a piece of dignity in this whole fiasco. "There's no smell of alcohol and he's not breathing. I checked his carotid artery for a pulse." She shrugged like a pro who thought this wasn't anything unusual. "Nothing there."

Not much to say to redeem herself from the near misstep. Except...she'd had the presence of mind to actually put on latex gloves before she'd opened the driver's-side door. That should count for something.

"Any signs of violence?" Lucas asked from directly behind her.

The darned man was dogging her steps like he needed to remain within *saving* distance. As if, at any moment she would make some stupid move and need his help again. What on earth was she going to do about him?

They arrived in the circle of lights beside the truck. "No," she answered, as she slowed her steps. "And since you're not a real officer of the law, you'd better stay back. Don't touch anything. Please."

Lucas grunted but stopped where he was. After flipping him a rolled-eyed look, she caught an expression in his eyes that stopped her, too. It appeared that, at least to him, she was the most competent FBI agent who had ever lived. The respectful gaze, full of admiration, threw her off balance yet again.

She didn't often see that kind of look in the expressions of the males around her. But when she spotted it on Lucas's face, her heart recognized the sentiment—and appreciated it maybe more than was totally proper.

Since she still had the gloves on, it was decided that she be the one to open the door wider so that they could more closely inspect the body. Kody seemed to be letting her take the lead in this investigation.

As another Special Agent who'd been in the field much longer, he was beginning to earn her respect and grateful admiration. And as for his cousin... Well, she still wasn't sure about the cousin.

The body was slumped over the steering wheel. It was hard to tell the dead man's age from this angle. About the only thing that could easily be seen was a wide back, clothed in a beige windbreaker. On closer inspection, though, he had on jeans, work boots and no hat. His hair appeared to be dark brown with no visible gray, but that wasn't always a good indicator of age.

"Strange," Kody said from over her shoulder. "Looks like he stopped here to rest and simply died. Let's take a few preliminary forensics photos before going any further. Okay, Special Agent?" He pulled a camera from his pack and snapped a couple of shots.

"Right," she said briskly. "Thanks. There sure don't seem to be any signs of violence. No blood. No damage to the windshield or vehicle. No obvious wounds. Maybe he had a heart attack."

"Perhaps a closer look, Special Agent?"

The words had come from Lucas and sent another chill down the back of her neck. Both she and Kody turned at the sound of his voice. Lucas's facial expression was grim. His whole body was tensed.

"What are you saying?"

"You are only seeing one view of this man's story. I had a dream of such a thing and believe there is more here to understand."

The FBI had full authority to investigate all unnatural deaths on federal reservations. If this was murder, it would be in Teal's jurisdiction.

She shrugged at Lucas's cryptic words and turned back to the man's body. She checked the jacket pockets, looking for ID, but came up empty. Then she took hold of the body by the shoulders and laid the man faceup across the front seat, with boots sticking out the door.

Sure enough, there it was. A small-caliber bullet hole—right smack in the middle of the guy's forehead.

"I'd say that looks plenty violent," Kody mumbled.

"Yeah," she reluctantly agreed. "I guess this is an official crime scene." Teal looked over her shoulder at Lucas and frowned. "Now I suppose I understand."

The first thing flashing in her mind was how Lucas Tso had known the way the man died. With the very few things she knew about him, though, she felt instinctively positive that Lucas could not be the one who shot this guy. No way.

But then, how had he known? Had he witnessed something before he saved her life that he wasn't telling? She was definitely not ready to concede Kody's statement that Lucas was some kind of psychic or fortune-teller. That idea was too crazy to contemplate.

"I've got crime scene tape in my pickup," Kody told her. "I'll go get it. I can call this in for you, too. If you want."

Nodding again, Teal wondered why Kody seemed so anxious to get away from her. The whole tense scene here at the truck was needlessly putting her nerves on edge.

She knew they were safe. Obviously, the murderer was long gone. In fact...

"Tell the office dispatcher that the dead man was killed somewhere else and the body was placed here," she called after Kody. "There's not enough blood around or in the truck for this to be the murder scene. He was shot, and probably cleaned up, then driven here for us to find. I'll want a forensic tech for both fingerprints and footprints, and I need a complete rundown on where this truck has been lately."

Kody nodded sharply and moved out of the light, heading back toward his pickup.

"Huh. He's sure acting odd all of a sudden," she mumbled to herself.

"Not really," Lucas said quietly from beside her. "Kody is acting perfectly normal for a Navajo."

"Do you mean he's upset that I'm taking the lead on this investigation? Is it because I'm a woman?"

"You don't know much about your own people, do you?"

"No. I suppose not."

"Your heritage will be important to you while you're on the reservation. Sometimes the difference between life and death. You need a few lessons. Shall I give you this one?"

She didn't want to be rude to him, but this was a murder investigation, and not the time for lessons. "Can I continue to check the body over while you talk?"

Turning her back with the hope that Lucas would keep quiet, she began patting down the body. She checked the man's pockets again and looked to see if anything might be hidden under the clothes.

Lucas hesitated only a few seconds before beginning his lecture. "Well, first off, the Dineh are a traditionally matriarchal society," he told her. "A Navajo would never begrudge a woman any position—especially not one of power. Kody wouldn't mind it if you were even his supervisor. That isn't how he was raised."

Mumbling as a response to Lucas's words, Teal went right on giving the scene a good once-over. She checked in the glove box and under the front seat. Except for an AAA map and a flashlight, the box was empty. Under the front seat she found a mess. She wondered about what other kinds of things might be under there with the thrown-away soda cups and the remnants of half-eaten burgers and fries.

A few minutes of fruitless searching later, and she'd

found nothing potentially dangerous. And she hadn't found identification to tell her who the dead man was, or even who the owner of the truck might be.

And unfortunately, there were no small-caliber weapons hidden around the place, either.

"Kody was not uncomfortable with *you*, but with the *body*," Lucas continued. "The Dineh have a long tradition and particular views about death and burials. Corpses are not for viewing. They're not even a subject for polite conversation." He said the words while keeping his distance, but he never turned away.

"Yes, I remember when my father died," she interrupted, but immediately wished she'd kept her mouth shut. There didn't seem to be any choice now but to explain. "When they recovered his body they buried him real quick. With very little ceremony."

"Recovered the body? How'd your father die?"

"Drowned." She'd said the word too bluntly and worried she should've seemed less intense. "I mean, he was a victim of a drowning accident. They had to send divers to look for his body."

Again there was a quiet moment when Lucas apparently took time to consider what had been said, and what he would say in response. But he surprised her with his next comment.

"Do you have one of those tiny plastic bag things used for collecting samples with you?"

"Huh? Why?" It was the first time in a while that she had turned her full attention to look at Lucas.

He was standing where she'd last seen him. His body language said he was composed and interested.

But he was studying her with an intensity that drove a spark up her spine.

So tall. So fine-looking, with all that dark hair and those stunning cheekbones…

But those weren't exactly the thoughts that an FBI special agent should be having in the middle of her investigation. Teal surreptitiously pinched her own thigh. Hard enough to bring tears to her eyes and her thoughts back around to the job at hand.

Lucas pointed to the man's boots. "Unusual things should be double-checked."

She opened her mouth to utter one more "huh?" but stopped and swallowed it back. Instead, she bent to study the filthy walking boots that were sticking out the door.

What was so unusual about a man wearing dirty boots? So the guy hadn't wasted the energy to polish them. So what?

It took a few minutes of staring at mud and stickers stuck to the edges of the man's soles for her to finally notice what she'd actually been seeing. The thing Lucas had wanted her to notice.

"The boots are muddy," she declared. "Where do you suppose he found mud to step in? It hasn't rained in weeks." Turning to Lucas for confirmation, she said. "At least not that I know of. Isn't that right?"

"It's been unusually dry for this time of year in Dinetah. And even if it had rained, the ground is so porous and rocky around here that the water drains off in a hurry."

Well, she guessed it was time for her to put aside

her aches and pains—and her insecurities—and really get down to work. It looked like this investigation was going to put her training to the test.

An hour later and two hundred miles north of Teal's crime scene, the dangerous and evil man who was known as the Navajo Wolf greeted one of his newest lieutenants. The Wolf followed the new man into the study of his favorite mansion—the one that sat high on a bluff of the Colorado Plateau overlooking the San Juan River.

It was all the Wolf could do to keep from grimacing at the sight of the new witch soldier who was currently wearing his Skinwalker persona. God, what a choice for the lieutenant to have made. A burrowing owl?

Despite the rumors of witchcraft that had surrounded the owl for generations, the damn thing was too—ugh—cute. Except for those piercing yellow eyes. They couldn't compare to the Navajo Wolf's legendary yellow eyes, of course, but they were credible enough for a Skinwalker witch soldier.

The Owl turned back into his humble and bumbling human form so he could talk to his boss. "Our operation is a success so far. It looks as though the FBI will be opening a full investigation at the coal mines now that a murder has been committed. And we've gotten lucky. At least two, and maybe more, of the Brotherhood appear to be interested in that murder, as well."

The Wolf tried to keep from barking his elation. "Excellent. We must have more diversions. That map, *my map,* disappeared somewhere along the river. Probably back in one of those caves. The Dog who thought he would steal it from me died before he could reveal his hiding place.

"But I feel that we're getting closer," the Wolf added with a twitch of his lips. "I don't want anyone interfering with our search. You keep circling the mine area. Continue looking out for the most damage and havoc you can cause."

"Yes, sir. But I'm having some trouble with the Bird People. No matter how unassuming I try to be in the air so I can hide, they always seem to know I'm not really one of them."

The Wolf gritted his teeth and stared down at his own hands. Cracked, raw and with the nails curling ever closer to real claws, his hands told the story he didn't want to admit. Even to himself. He was losing control.

It had gotten so bad lately that every time he changed over from his human form, he came back sicker and sicker. His skin was permanently pockmarked, his heart raced whenever he lay down. And his mind...

Few memories remained. But memory was of no consequence. He growled, snapping his jaw with a sneer.

The map. If he didn't get his hands on the map, someone would pay. He knew the elusive map would ultimately lead him to the rest of the parchments. He was absolutely sure of it.

And the sacred parchments held the final secrets

that the Skinwalkers must have. The keys to unlocking the ancient chants and potions necessary for their eternal life. And those same parchments would cure them of the physical afflictions currently plaguing all the Skinwalkers whenever they changed form too often.

He waved away the Owl's nonsensical objections and nearly bit the bird's head off. "Do whatever you have to. And keep using the more Anglo-styled weapons for your diversions. Like pistols and dynamite. The very things that will make the Brotherhood believe their trouble has nothing to do with us.

"In fact," he continued, grinding out his evil demands. "Infiltrate one of the environmental protest groups that are causing minor troubles around the mines. Those amateur ecoterrorists should be thrilled to have a real Navajo join their cause. Maybe we can use them to our advantage."

The Owl agreed and quickly left. No one wanted to be in the presence of the crazed Navajo Wolf for very long.

Well, the Owl was an idiot. A necessary idiot for the time being, perhaps. But ultimately he was expendable. The entire army of Skinwalkers would be expendable. The Wolf didn't need any of them and would gladly find a way to get rid of them all when the time came.

All he needed…all he could concentrate on anymore…was locating that damned map.

The ambulance carrying the body bag had long

since gone, along with the agents, paramedics and technicians who'd been dragged out of their beds to come to the scene. Even Kody had finally headed home in the early hours of morning.

Teal stayed behind, waiting for daylight and the clean-up forensics team to show up to finish gathering evidence and haul the truck away to their impound facility. When she had simply refused to leave, wanting to take no chance of letting anyone or anything destroy evidence at her crime scene, Lucas remained behind, too.

"You didn't have to stay with me," she said irritably. Lucas was sitting next to her on the flat rock. "I am *not* your responsibility. I'm perfectly capable of taking care of myself."

"Of course you are," he said as amicably as possible.

He didn't want to argue with her. He wanted them to become friends. There was some predestined reason he'd been dreaming about her since the age of twelve, and he was determined to find out why before he let her out of his sight for very long.

His gut told him he was meant to save her life, probably from a Skinwalker attack. That had to be the reason he'd dreamed of her for so many years.

It was still the dark of night. The hours right before dawn were always the most dangerous for Skinwalker activity. He would never have allowed her to stay out here alone before daylight.

They sat for a few minutes in an uncomfortable silence. Lucas realized he wasn't hearing her thoughts anymore. But at least she couldn't still be afraid of him. He was positive he'd be able to see an obvious emotion like fear in her eyes.

"Well, then, why don't you go ahead and leave already?" she suddenly blurted out in a most annoyed tone. She was swiping angrily at the hair in her face.

Obviously still in pain, and also just as obviously frustrated with her body's dusty condition, Teal was letting irritation color the words she chose.

He nearly laughed aloud as he watched her fighting phantom flyaway hairs. Every time she stuffed a recalcitrant ebony strand behind her ear, the silky soft ends slipped back down over her eyes. It was everything he could do not to touch it—touch her.

But he managed to sit there without moving and without saying a word. The FBI special agent would not care for him to be so familiar just yet. They weren't even friends.

"Talk about your ultimate in bad hair days," she groaned, apparently forgetting for the moment her desire to be rid of him. "I am so filthy, all I can think of is getting into a shower."

"Except for the few bruises and cuts, you look great," he soothed. "In fact, better than great. You're one of the most exotic and beautiful women I've ever met."

Teal twisted her head and shot him an incredulous look. "Skip the phony flattery. I know what I look like, and it's not great.

"I have a younger sister," she added without a breath. "She's the pretty one in the family. I'm plain old

Teal. I've always thought of myself as just one of the guys."

That brought to his mind another question he certainly wished he could read in her eyes. Hours ago he'd stopped being able to read Teal's thoughts at all. It was a strange feeling this—not knowing. Strange and alarming.

"I can't imagine you actually believe such nonsense," he said with a wry smile. "Aren't the men in your life forever telling you how pretty you are?"

She dropped her hands into her lap. "Is that a sneaky way of asking about my personal life? Are you flirting?"

He couldn't keep the grin from spreading across his face. "And that would be so terrible, because...?"

Shrugging, she turned her face away so he couldn't see her eyes.

The woman sitting next to him was more than simply pretty. She was beyond beautiful. With those huge chocolate-colored eyes and those long lashes skimming her cheeks every time she looked down, Special Agent Teal Benaly radiated sensuality. And somehow, it ceased mattering that he had no idea what she was thinking.

Finally she turned back. "I'm single. Not involved with anyone, either, if you must know. But that doesn't mean I can take the time to date or start a new relationship at the moment."

"Not with anyone?" he asked. "Or just not with me?"

"Not with anyone. But thanks for asking."

She was being flip, but he heard an emotion in her voice that made his heart stutter. He wanted to know more about her. Like for instance, what had that achingly familiar but not quite clear tone of voice really meant?

"Maybe if you got to know me better, I could change your mind." He watched her expression carefully.

It was difficult not being in tune with her thoughts. Unaccustomed to the absence of noise in his head, he had to keep a close watch on her eyes and body movements to guess what she was thinking.

However, her current thoughts seemed easy enough to judge. She screwed up her mouth and stared at him as if she, too, were trying to guess what he'd been thinking.

Then she lifted a shoulder and sighed as though she'd temporarily given up. "Kody told me you're an athlete. Is that right?"

Lucas didn't think that was what she'd meant to ask, but he answered her question anyway. "Yes, that's right. Every year but this one, I've placed in the top ten in the Iron Man competition." He shrugged himself. "It's something I love to do."

"Iron Man, huh? I've heard that's a bitch. How come you didn't place this year?"

"I decided not to compete. Things were...well, things around Dinetah were complicated this year. I had a lot going on."

"A lot going on? Let me guess. Does it have to do with...a woman?"

Ah. The question she had hesitated to ask before.

"Isn't that too personal a question for a woman who doesn't want a relationship?" he teased.

She shrugged and smiled a wry grin. "I'm allowed to wonder about personal things, too. But I have a better reason to ask than you do. It's in my job description."

He chuckled. "I'm divorced, Special Agent. And before your next too-personal question, it was a long time ago and there were no children. I live alone—about a half mile from my grandmother's hogan where I was raised."

It hit him then that most of the time he felt very much alone. But that was his choice now. He'd come to terms with his life.

Teal watched the quiet struggle behind Lucas's eyes over that last sentence. But she had no idea what he'd said that was so difficult for him to admit or accept.

This guy absolutely fascinated her. She couldn't tell what he meant half the time. She'd always prided herself on being able to read people's intentions, figuring it was one of the things that would make her excel in law enforcement. But with him...*nada*.

As she continued to watch him, his face became bathed in an eerie rose glow. Turning, she discovered the first few rays of sun creeping over the rim of a canyon.

"Sunrise," Lucas said with a smile. "Things in the desert take on a different hue at first light. See how the gray sand is now cast in pinks and golds?"

"You have a real artistic temperament, don't you?"

He nodded, but didn't say anything more while he

continued to stare up at the soft colors of the morning sky at dawn. Teal was beginning to feel a comradeship, or a kind of familiarity with him, and she wasn't at all sure she wanted to. The guy was a flirt and a weirdo.

But he seemed like a loner, and she was most definitely a loner, too. Though the idea that they were both single and each stayed to themselves didn't seem like much to build a friendship around.

In spite of the fact he was sexy as hell and that should be enough all by itself to keep her interest, there was something else about him that seemed to be drawing her, or calling to her. A nebulous thing, right outside of her conscious, she was determined to figure out what it was.

"I'd like to say a few sunrise prayers," he told her softly. "It's something I do every day. Would you mind?"

She jumped to her feet, stung by her own wayward thoughts. "No. Not at all. The forensics team will be here soon anyway." She started off toward the crime scene tape and the abandoned truck, eager to get away from him for a few minutes and give him some peace.

"Wait."

Not wanting to hang around to face her self-examinations while he prayed, she moved faster. "I'll go stand by the truck, don't worry about…"

"Teal, stop moving."

The tone of his voice told her there was trouble. But her feet didn't get the message. She couldn't stop the forward motion, but turned her head back around to check on what he'd wanted to say.

Lucas was racing toward her, already only a foot away. "Stop," he shouted as he reached his arms out for her.

"Huh?"

But it was too late to stop. Her back foot was slipping off the edge of some precipice.

Damn it. She'd been there, done this. And how did a frigging cliff suddenly appear on flat ground anyhow?

Her balance was definitely lost. She tried to save herself, and grabbed for Lucas. He was strong—and could be her savior once again.

Which was her very last thought as she started backwards over a dark edge. This time, though, she'd hooked her arms around Lucas and took him along.

Both of them went flying off into oblivion—together.

# Chapter 4

Lucas wrapped his arms around her and twisted his body before they hit the ground. He'd been aware Teal was about to step into the prairie dogs' city, but he couldn't reach her in time to stop her fall. He'd hit one of the holes in his haste and lost his balance, too.

All he could do now was tuck and roll, keeping her body cushioned with his own. He landed flat on his back, and finally stopped rolling with the special agent's inert body splayed like a broken doll across his chest.

The gorgeous special agent of his dreams. This couldn't be good news for their budding relationship.

"You okay?" he whispered when his breath evened out.

Teal remained quiet, not even stirring in his arms.

Did she have the breath knocked out of her? Was she conscious?

Afraid to move, afraid not to, Lucas held his breath and waited a minute. Finally, he felt her chest heaving in and out and knew at least she was breathing.

He loosened his grip, and with a sigh of tremendous relief softly placed his lips against her silken hair. She was okay.

Squirming slightly in his arms, she ended up aligning her limp body exactly horizontally with his. He cursed under his breath. His body immediately reacted to the movements and to the feel of a rounded female pressing against him too intimately. Instead of limp, he went hard. Completely normal for a healthy male. But not so good for someone who was trying to earn her trust.

He could feel her warm breath against the damp skin of his neck, and chills began nipping along his spine. His heart raced as he felt her nipples pebble into his chest.

Lucas began to shake. His body wanted one thing—desperately. But his head knew better than to let anything like that happen between them. Not yet.

"Please," he begged. "You have to get up. It wouldn't do your career any good for the forensic team to show up and find us rolling around in the sand together."

That seemed to get through to her. She groaned and slid off his body to the ground beside him.

The sound and friction of her movements melted his insides and hardened other parts. "Talk to me, Teal. Are you injured?"

"How the hell did a cliff come out of nowhere like that? I thought..." She lifted her head and looked around. "What happened?"

"You stepped into a prairie dog hole and lost your balance. You didn't twist your ankle, did you?"

She sat up and checked both her ankles. "I guess not. In fact, I seem to be in remarkably good shape. Is that thanks to you?"

Lucas sat up beside her, hoping the lingering shadows of dawn would hide the evidence of his own body's shape. At least until he could get things back under control.

"It wasn't anything. I gave you something to land on."

"That's twice you've saved my life. I owe you big time."

"I would hardly call tripping over a hole in the desert a matter of life and death. As long as you're okay..." He stopped himself from finishing. Would it be better to have her feeling obligated to him? Could that work in his favor?

He clamped his mouth shut and shrugged. "We'll work something out."

Standing, he held out his hand. "Let me help you up. Go slowly until you're sure no bones are broken."

"I'm fine," she said with a grunt as she got to her feet. "Just embarrassed. I'm usually pretty agile. I don't know what's the matter with me."

"Don't be too hard on yourself. You're in a strange land and unfamiliar with the environment." He watched as she dusted off her slacks and jacket. "This might be a sign, you know."

She lifted her eyebrows in question.

"You're going to need someone to watch over you until you learn your way around. There's a lot of hidden dangers in the high desert. Maybe…"

"Are you applying for the job?" Her voice carried an angry note of sarcasm, and he figured he'd pushed her too fast after all.

"Teal. I'm just saying you could use some help. Temporarily, of course. I'd be willing to…"

"Forget it. The FBI would not approve of one of their special agents needing a bodyguard. It's against regulation."

Lucas dropped the subject. But he had to find a way to stay close to her. Teal could potentially be in danger from things she didn't even know existed. And he was positive it would somehow be his destiny to keep her safe.

He considered his options for a moment. Now that he thought about it, she'd given him a good idea. Perhaps there was a way to make the FBI change at least one of their regulations.

Teal flipped her cell phone closed and groaned. Slowly sliding her way to a sitting position at the side of the bed, she tried to ignore the fact that every inch of her body hurt.

Now that she was beginning to wake up, yesterday's activities seemed like a big blur. Although after leaving Many Caves Canyon in late midmorning, she definitely remembered going to the medical examiner's office to check on when they could do the autopsy, and she also vaguely remembered going back to the field office in Farmington to transcribe her notes on the murder scene. But the rest of the day was still a little fuzzy.

Except... Her memories of every minute with Lucas were entirely too sharp and clear.

She'd finally gotten rid of him when she managed to hitch a ride back to her car with the forensic techs. But the damned strange man continued to occupy a huge part of both her waking thoughts and her nighttime dreams.

Taking a breath and steeling herself for the pain, she got to her feet. Thank goodness she wasn't lightheaded this morning. Not when her boss had just called and wanted her in his office for a meeting within the hour.

Better get a move on. Struggling on her shaky and bruised legs into the tiny bathroom of her rented mobile home, she flipped on the harsh overhead light and glanced at herself in the mirror.

Big mistake. With a sharp gasp, Teal stared openmouthed at somebody else's image gazing back at her. Just look at that poor woman's face. It looked like someone had stuck her head in a washing machine full of rocks and punched the spin cycle.

Now wasn't that attractive? How was she ever going to be able to act like a professional in front of her boss with a black eye, a puffy, red nose and that nasty dirty bandage on her cheek? She looked like a boxer after losing a fight.

There was no choice in the matter, however. Special Agent In Charge Sullivan had summoned her and she had to go. Maybe she could cover up some of the damage with makeup.

Pulling the tiny butterfly bandage off her cheek, she found the cut underneath looked almost healed. Was fast healing one of the effects of Lucas's medicine-man salve? She glanced down at the back of her hands and was surprised to see that the cuts there looked better, too. Something had made a tremendous difference overnight.

Okay, time to quit daydreaming and get moving. She was becoming more and more curious about what her boss wanted with her. Today was supposed to be her day off, though she'd planned to do a few preliminary interviews for her murder investigation.

Looking in the medicine cabinet for some way to cover the bruises, she ended up chuckling at her own dumb ideas. Makeup? At FBI Special Agent Teal Benaly's place? *Puleeez*. She'd be lucky to find a lipstick.

Instead she spotted a bottle of peroxide and hurriedly splashed it over her hands and face. After two minutes of whimpering over the pains she'd inflicted upon herself, Teal ran a wet toothbrush around the inside of her mouth—carefully. Then she tried brushing her clean but still matted hair.

Hobbling back to her bedroom, she threw open her closet looking for a nice pair of black slacks to wear to the office. Again, a moment's reflection reminded her that she hadn't done laundry in a couple of weeks.

She rummaged through the dirty clothes basket and came up with slacks that had only one tiny spot of spilled coffee on them. Coffee against black material? No one would notice. These would have to do. Easing into them, she considered a top and decided to go with a pullover sweater that she hadn't worn yet this season. It was bound to be clean. She gave the armpits the old sniff test then pulled it over her head.

On her way out the door, Teal stopped and dumped a lump of fish food into the glass bowl with her Japanese fighting fish. "That ought to do you, Hiro. Sorry I can't stay and join you for breakfast," she murmured as she locked the front door behind her.

What had ever possessed her to buy a fish, anyway? She'd never had any kind of pets before. Living things just seemed so difficult. You couldn't quantify them, and they tended to get messy sometimes.

But she'd felt really isolated when she'd first come to the reservation. Actually, she'd been lonely for a long while before that, but out here in this odd world the loneliness seemed magnified.

And really, Hiro was hardly any trouble. He was hardly any company, either, but she was glad for him just the same.

Outside in the sunshine, she discovered getting into her car was a real trick without bumping into any of her major bruises. After issuing a few audible grunts and groans, she finally made it behind the wheel. And with only fifteen minutes left to make it to the field office, she spun her wheels and squealed out of the driveway.

Sixteen minutes later, Teal wheeled into the parking lot of the federal administrative offices in Farmington and parked in her regular spot. She gritted her teeth, jumped free of the car instead of prolonging the agony, and limped into FBI headquarters for the upper New Mexico/Arizona reservation area.

Passing by the series of cubbyhole desks in the outer office, she ignored the stares and comments of the assistants and secretaries. For once in her life, she had nothing to say and couldn't even manage to make her aching body shrug in answer to the questions about her bruises.

After knocking, she was invited into her boss's office but was surprised to see two Navajo men sitting in the brown leather wingback chairs in front of his desk. Her boss, Special Agent In Charge Chris Sullivan, gave her a wide-eyed once-over, but waved her to a side chair as both the Navajo men turned to stare at her face.

"Special Agent Benaly, I'd like you to meet Councilman Ayze of the Navajo Nation Tribal Council." Chris seemed willing to ignore her appearance, saying nothing as he indicated the more well-dressed and older of the two men.

Teal nodded and tried a weak smile. But since the gray-haired gentleman made no move to stand or shake her hand, she folded her arms across her waist and tried to fade into the carpet.

The younger of the two men stood then and came over to shake her hand. "Nice to meet you, Agent

Benaly. I'm Ernest Sam, acting director of the Navajo Department of Public Safety. I understand you have been briefed on the problems we've been having out in the Black Mesa mine area?"

Slipping her hand free of his grip, she answered, "Yes, Director Sam, I have been. But at the moment I'm trying to make a connection between the murdered man we found in Many Caves Canyon and the troubles around the mine."

"The young man who died was my assistant," Councilman Ayze cut in without really turning to look at her. "He was also the son of a favored cousin on my Water's Edge Clan side. A good man. A good husband and father."

"I'm sorry to hear that." Teal turned to her boss for confirmation.

"Eddie Cohoe was the man's name," Chris told her. "His wife identified his body late last night."

"The one who died had called the councilman on the day he disappeared," Director Sam began soberly. "He was agitated, but said he couldn't explain over the phone. Councilman Ayze cleared his schedule for the next morning to meet with him, but the assistant never showed."

Teal couldn't help but notice that neither Navajo man seemed willing to say the name of the deceased. She'd been warned of that particular tradition by the ME yesterday. It made her wonder what other traditions she might not know that could get her into real trouble with these two important men.

"Well," she hesitated, unwilling to say the wrong thing. "Uh, thank you for…"

Mercifully Chris interrupted her. "Cohoe was the first one to notice the troubling new conspiracy going on inside the ranks of the environmentalists around the Navajo mine area. He convinced the Tribal Council to ask for federal help, and he believed the seemingly un-related accidents around the mines were really acts of terrorism made to look fairly benign. I understand he'd recently been trying to gather information on the eco-groups' leaders."

"The one who died suggested that he be allowed to accompany the FBI's new man on his investigations," Director Sam told her. "He had made some inroads with the environmentalists and thought he could advise the FBI on the Navajo way.

"When we originally asked the feds for help," the director continued, "we'd wanted them to send someone who would be unfamiliar to the environmen-talists. But we'd hoped the person would also be Dineh so the People would feel comfortable talking to him."

"I see." Teal was becoming decidedly uncomfort-able with the direction of this conversation. Was she about to be replaced?

"But no one is left who knows what my assistant's research would show." The councilman swung his gaze over her battered body and wrinkled clothes with a scowl.

"I can get up to speed in a hurry," Teal said in her own defense.

Director Sam smiled at her. "We would like to

continue with the original plan of having a traditionalist accompany the FBI, if at all possible. Luckily, a traditionalist has volunteered to be your teacher and to accompany you in your investigations in Dinetah. He—"

"Who?" The idea didn't sound good to her at all.

"Apparently, the Navajo Nation has several, uh, *sensitives* among their number," Chris said while trying to hide his spreading grin. "They have found a man who can read minds and who is willing to travel along and be your guide during your investigations."

Oh, hell. She tried to say something that wouldn't be taken the wrong way, but choked. There was no way she would be willing to—

"The young sensitive's gifts will be able to make up for the one who died's lost information," Councilman Ayze said. "We are grateful that this busy man has the time available to help the Nation, though the Tribal Council has long been aware of his dedication to the People."

No frigging way. Uh-uh. "The man's name wouldn't by any chance be…"

"Lucas Tso," the director cut in with a grin. "He's quite famous. You may have seen some of his art."

She opened her mouth, thought about it and pressed her lips together again.

"Actually, I understand the special agent has already met the sensitive," Councilman Ayze said through his own wry grin. "Lucas Tso is one of my wife's nephews. He tells me that he was with this woman lawman in Many Caves Canyon when she discovered the body."

Trapped. That damned Lucas had worked some

kind of magic on all of these men and she would be the one to end up paying for it.

Her eyes glazed over and she barely heard the rest of the conversation, but within a few minutes, she had been ordered to work with and listen to the one guy she had hoped she wouldn't run into again for a good long while.

Finally dismissed, Teal managed to make a quiet exit from her boss's office. Shaking her head as she came through the door, she tried to get a handle on what had just happened to her. She swiped a palm across her sweaty brow and looked over to the first assistant's desk she could see, hoping to find one of her favorite secretaries whose shoulder she could cry on.

But there instead, leaning his butt against the edge of the desk and watching her closely, was the man of the hour. He sure looked cool and composed, too. Which made her sweat more than ever.

His chambray shirtsleeves were rolled up, exposing powerful forearms crossed over his wide chest. Barely able to stand seeing the appreciative expression in his eyes as he watched her, she quickly took in the rest of his appearance instead. Soft but expensive jeans encased his thighs. But maybe that wasn't where she should be looking, either. Her eyes moved hurriedly down his legs to feet that were also crossed casually at the ankles, mimicking his arms. And those feet were encased in well-worn but clean working boots, making him look even more masculine and sexy.

Head to toe, the irritating man looked good enough to eat.

"Lucas Tso, what the hell have you done?"

"Me? I have no clue what you mean, Special Agent."

Teal stormed over and punched his shoulder. "You hypnotized Councilman Ayze and convinced him to insist I needed you to be my guide. Didn't you?"

He tried to stem the grin that threatened. She wouldn't like it if she thought he was laughing at her. And he wasn't laughing at her at all.

His whole body was smiling at the way her eyes sparked with anger and at how the energy was fairly snapping around her. She looked sexy, despite her crumpled and bruised appearance, and the sight of her made him weak in the knees.

"Not at all," he managed to say calmly. "I have no idea how to hypnotize a person. That's not an art I've mastered. What's more, the councilman himself was the one who suggested I'd be the right person for the job."

Lucas watched her clamp her teeth together.

Growling under her breath, she spun around and stomped toward the front lobby.

Starting out after her, Lucas followed her through the narrow aisles. But within a few seconds he spotted her limping, favoring the knee he knew she'd injured in her fall. A knife of sympathy twisted in his gut.

He waited until she stepped out into the privacy and sunshine of the parking lot before he caught up to her. "Hold on a second, Bright Eyes."

She turned away from him. "Go away."

Forced to take her arm in order to keep her still, he tried to be as gentle as possible. "Teal, wait. Your boss gave you a direct order to work with me. Don't let your emotions ruin your career."

As she rounded on him, he saw the pain etched on her face. He dropped his hand and moved closer.

"The aching is bad, isn't it?" he asked in a whisper.

Taking a deep breath, she straightened her spine. "That's none of your business."

He picked up both of her hands and turned them over to check out the backsides. "The cut on your face is better, and the nicks on your hands are almost healed. It was my salve which performed that magic. Do you remember when I told you I also have another kind of medicine that will take away some of your aches—like the one in your knee?"

Her eyes narrowed, but she nodded.

"I don't have it with me today. But if you'll accompany me to my grandmother's hogan, she makes those kinds of medicine and she'll be able to help you."

Teal scowled, but Lucas could tell she was in enough pain to be ready to try almost anything. "We have to work and travel together from now on anyway. Why not start trusting me today?"

"It's my day off." The way she said the words let him know this would be her last minor objection.

In the Navajo Way, he waited, saying nothing.

"Is it very far?" she asked quietly.

"About an hour's drive. I thought I'd follow you home so you can leave your car and come with me. It's kind of tricky finding the place. I know the shortcuts and my SUV is four-wheel drive."

She stood tentatively and with her shoulders hunched against the pain. It was all he could do not to sweep her up and cart her off for help. The look of anguish in her eyes was killing him.

"Please, partner," he pleaded. "Let me do this for you. We can talk about the case on the way, if you like."

The mention of work seemed to break her icy indecision.

"Fine," she said with something that looked like relief in her eyes. "But I'm bringing my weapon along, too. Just in case."

Knowing he needed to break the tension, Lucas tried a little humor. "Why, Special Agent love, you can't mean you think you might need to use it on *moi?*" Bowing with a flourish of his hand, he watched her expression relax.

He gently took her elbow and began guiding her toward her standard-issue sedan. "Don't I recall you saying just yesterday that you owed me big-time? I haven't yet made up my mind what you can do to pay me back, but I don't think shooting me or my grandmother will be high on the list."

"Oh...I...I..." She blinked and looked embarrassed.

"I'm teasing you, Bright Eyes. Relax. If you feel better wearing your gun, by all means bring it along."

Guns were not the weapon of choice for Skinwalkers—or for the Brotherhood. But if they ran into any

## Chapter 5

"You have a pet fish?" Lucas turned the key in his transmission and pulled out onto the major highway in front of Teal's mobile home.

For the last fifteen minutes he'd been waiting in her living room for Teal to change into more comfortable jeans and a sweatshirt. After changing, Teal had grabbed her notebook, cell phone and Glock, then locked everything before letting him help ease her into the passenger seat of his extratall SUV. Funny that her body aches were so much worse than yesterday.

"Not just any fish," she answered after finding a comfortable spot. "A Japanese fighting fish. His name is Hiro."

"Do you own any other pets?"

She tried to shake her head, but felt a grinding ache

down her neck. Checking out Lucas's profile, she realized he was gazing through the windshield and wouldn't have seen her movement in any case.

"No," she mumbled. "Just Hiro. Do you own any pets?"

"Traditional Navajos don't own domesticated animals. If we have them in our homes, it's usually because they chose us."

"Okey-dokie, then," she said with a roll of her eyes. "But that's no answer. Do you have a pet?"

"There is a cat who lives with me. A *bilagaana* cat named *Yas*—Snow. But…"

"A what-kind-of cat?" she interrupted him to ask.

"A *white man's* cat. An Anglo cat."

"A white man's cat? As opposed to a *Navajo* cat? What's the difference, and how did you get an Anglo cat?"

Lucas didn't answer right away and she glanced over to check on him again. He was busy guiding the SUV off the main highway and onto a long, straight two-lane road. His jaw was tight, and she tried not to watch as the muscles in his powerful arms rolled and bunched while he turned the wheel.

Whew, baby. Squirming in her seat, Teal decided to concentrate her attention out the window. Their SUV was now heading directly down the long, narrow road toward the closest mountain range.

On the map back in the glove box of her car, she vaguely remembered these mountains were marked as the Chuska Range. Today they were shrouded in a hazy purple overcast, and looked like ghost peaks.

Huh? What a whimsical thing for her to think. She was much more a reality kind of girl. Must be the pains. They needed to hurry up and get to his grandmother's house.

"Snow was my ex-wife's cat," he finally said. "She acquired him during her last year at UCLA. I think it was her roommate who'd been giving out the kittens. Anyway, my ex-wife couldn't resist the tiny ball of black fur.

"When she left me and went back to L.A. to live, the cat stayed. By that time, Snow was notably resistible."

"So, because he was born off the reservation, that makes him an Anglo cat?"

Lucas chuckled low in his throat and threw her a smile. "That's part of it. But more so because my ex-wife pampered him and refused to let him go outside to hunt or do his business. She's the one who made him more Anglo than Navajo. I think the cat would've fit in nicely if she'd only given him a chance."

Teal got the picture. Lucas thought a Navajo cat should be an outdoors cat. Hunting and fishing and foraging for his own food. But their discussion had made her curious about a few more things.

"Was your ex-wife an Anglo woman?"

That got another chuckle out of Lucas. "Full-blooded Navajo by birth. Anglo by design. After she came home from college, she couldn't wait for the time when she would be able to leave Dinetah again."

Uncomfortable with the subject of wanting to get away from the reservation, Teal nevertheless decided to push him for more details. She and Lucas were never going to be lovers, let alone get married. It didn't matter that she and his ex-wife shared the same dislike of Navajoland, even if being like her had been slightly shocking at first.

But *he'd* been the one who'd wanted them to be friends. So he could damn well suck it up and answer all of Teal's personal questions. Asking embarrassing things was part of her job. He'd forced his way into her investigation, and he would have to learn to take whatever came with it.

"Is that why the two of you divorced? She wanted to live in a big city off the reservation and you didn't?"

Never taking his eyes off the road ahead, Lucas pursed his lips for a second before he answered. "Things are seldom that simple between two people, Bright Eyes. I know you prefer your answers to be in black and white, but human relationships usually fall more into shades of gray."

What kind of half-assed answer was that? "Did she love you?"

The minute that question was out of her mouth, Teal knew she'd stepped over some invisible boundary. And what's more, it had been a stupid question and not even in good interrogator's style. Her trainer in interrogations class back at Quantico would probably be cringing right now.

"Yes, I think she did." Lucas answered the totally rude question without hesitation. He didn't seem to mind that such a question was far too personal to be asked of near strangers like the two of them.

"Or, at least, she did at first," he hedged.

Okay, *now* a zillion thoughts were bouncing around in her head. Did his wife stop loving him when she discovered he was a "sensitive" weirdo? Or had she married a famous artist, hoping for the money and prestige, only to get a man who could read her thoughts and was considered strange by his own family and friends?

But Teal had made up her mind to stop asking about things when she might not want the answers. She turned her head to stare out the window at the interesting scenery and kept her mouth shut. It was all she could do to keep the pain at bay this morning, let alone sort through crazy thoughts that had less to do with her assignment and more to do with a sexy sensitive who owned a black cat named Snow.

Their SUV was passing through an immense flat and dry land, and the scenery was not terribly compelling, with its murky colors of dove-gray and pale tan. She'd seen a few sheep, though there had been no fences. And every once in a while, a driveway seemed to pop up out of nowhere.

Eventually, she became interested in the way almost every driveway entry seemed to be marked by old tires on wooden posts. "What are the tires for?"

"It's one way of finding the right driveway, even in the snow. Navajo traditionalists don't believe in using proper names. So you generally won't see names painted on mailboxes or those cute ranch names on signposts like Texas ranchers sometimes use."

"I thought…" She hesitated, then decided to ask

him anyway. That's what he'd volunteered for, right? "Someone told me not using names is the tradition when it comes to talking about dead people. You mean Navajos can't use anyone's name ever?"

Lucas threw her a quick smile. "You have to remember when you're out talking to the People in Dinetah that there are at least three distinct divisions among them these days. There are the traditionalists..."

"Like you?"

"There are a growing number of young people who have chosen to follow the Way, yes. And there's a big push to teach the language and the traditions to the children. But most of the true traditionalists are elderly now.

"Then there are the Dineh who were converted to Christianity by missionaries years ago," he continued. "And finally, there are many Navajo who refer to themselves as modern. I'm not exactly sure they have any philosophy that is truly their own. So, in other words, some Navajos have no problem with using proper names and others do."

He'd wandered off the subject, but that was okay. There seemed to be so many basics for her to learn.

"I need a better explanation."

He smiled sheepishly. "Traditional Dineh believe it is rude to use proper names. So, as children, we're given secret warrior names by an elder of our clan and sometimes we're also given nicknames by our friends or families. Not all of us use the childhood names, however. Mostly, we just go by our relationship names. You know, like *Son, Mother, Cousin*. It's easier."

"I get that. But what's so rude about using the name of a dead person who can't hear what you say about him?"

"That's a whole other lesson for another time. Remember our talk about Kody and the murder victim? There's quite a few Dineh traditions about death and killing. And I'm not sure you're in good enough shape for learning much more today. How's the pain?"

"Not too bad." But every time she moved she knew that statement was a lie.

"Relax. We're nearly there. Only fifteen or twenty more miles. Can you make it?"

Teal nodded and closed her eyes. She tried to think about how best to go about her inquiries into the murder, but ended up wondering what Lucas was thinking about instead. He was awfully quiet.

About ten minutes later Lucas turned the SUV yet again, this time off the asphalt onto a gravel road that seemed to lead upward into a section of pine-green hills. He hadn't said a word in fifteen minutes. It made her nervous.

"Have you ever been in love, Bright Eyes?" he asked at last.

She deserved that one and should've seen it coming. It was only fair that she give him as honest an answer as he'd given her to a nosy question.

"No, I guess I can't really say that I have. I was in-fatuated once and thought I was madly in love—for at least two whole weeks. And I have definitely been in lust—a couple of times. But real love? Nope."

Lucas kept his thoughts to himself and appeared to be concentrating on the road ahead. Which was probably just as well from her point of view. What more needed to be said from either of them about the subject of love and marriage?

Besides, if he wanted any more personal answers, he could darn well read her mind to get them.

Lucas downshifted at the top of a familiar rise. Not much further now. For a moment he wished he could become one of the unnaturally evil, like the Skinwalkers, so he could use his supernatural powers and fly Teal the rest of the way to his grandmother's, though he knew such ideas were wrong to consider.

But even without being able to read her thoughts, he'd felt Teal's suffering. He knew of her pains, not by hearing them in his mind the way he used to, but by the manner in which she cringed at every bump in the road and winced whenever she needed to shift around in her seat.

She was being so brave and trying to be so tough. It was killing him.

Remembering back to the hundreds of nights he had dreamed of her, Lucas would've known that much about her anywhere. But what he hadn't known was how he would feel about it when faced with the reality. Every ache of hers stabbed at his heart. Every pain was magnified a million times in his own limbs.

He hadn't saved her from suffering when it mattered the most. At least, not the way he had many times in his dreams.

When he'd asked her about ever being in love, he'd hoped, or maybe even expected, to hear her tell him about a dream lover. A lean, athletic man who for years had come to her side during long lonely nights. But her answer had been nothing like what he'd wanted to hear. Hadn't Teal ever dreamed of him the way he had dreamed of her?

Worse by far than feeling her pains in his own body, Lucas was actually beginning to worry that he might not be the right man for the job of protecting her in Navajoland. Over the last thirty-six hours, her presence had been blocking most of the noises he'd heard in his head ever since he could remember. The thoughts from Teal's mind had disappeared almost immediately after he'd realized who she really was. But over the last few hours, the thoughts of others had also begun to fade away.

A forgotten series of gravel grates in the road a few miles from his grandmother's hogan caused the SUV to jolt as it went over the bumps. Lucas slashed a fast glance over to the woman in the passenger seat. Her eyes were closed, but he saw pain etched in her face, causing tight little lines around her eyes and mouth. He vowed to be more careful, but the boulders on each side of the road pretty much precluded him from avoiding the worst of the ruts.

In the absence of Teal's thoughts, Lucas's own thoughts went back to the circumstances of losing his gift. He'd always considered the psychic gift of foresight as more of a burden than a pleasure. And many times in his life he'd wished it would just go away. That he would wake up completely normal someday.

His *amá sání* had the gift, too, and her life had never been easy. But she'd never felt singled out and remote by being a stargazer, the way he had as a child.

In the last few years though, he'd found a place to belong amongst the Brotherhood, with cousins and clansmen who did not judge him. And what's more, they needed him and his talents. He was their equal in the Skinwalker war. He'd contributed. He'd mattered to people in a personal way and not just as an artistic talent or the weirdo clansman.

What would the Brotherhood think of him when they discovered his talents were gone? What could he do for them then?

Grinding the gears one last time in order to top the hill and dip down into his *amá sání's* meadow, Lucas nearly cried out with relief. Teal would soon be getting the help she needed to conquer her pain.

But he would have little part in the cure. He could stand guard over her, yes. But when it was important, when he should've been there for her, once more he was going to be the odd man out.

The strange guy who didn't fit in.

Teal felt the SUV come to a stop and she opened her eyes. Lucas had parked in front of one of those eight-sided buildings she'd noticed from a distance during her travels around the reservation. But up close, this one looked homey, with curtains in the windows and smoke coming from a pipe in the center of the roof.

"Is this where your grandmother lives?" She reached for the door handle.

Lucas lightly put his hand on her shoulder. "We need to give it a few minutes. Navajos wait to be invited inside."

"Another tradition?" His hand was warm and slightly tingling as it lay against her sweatshirt.

"Yes," he said and removed his hand.

Teal felt the absence of warmth like a shot of ice water.

"It's meant to give the People in remote areas a chance to decide whether they wish to have visitors or not," he added. "There are still plenty of distant places on the reservation that do not have electricity or phone service."

"Isn't your grandmother expecting us?"

"I gave her a cell phone a few years ago, in case of emergencies. And I called before we left your house to tell her we were on the way. But still, we must wait."

The front door opened at that moment and an ancient-looking woman stepped across the threshold. She raised her hand slightly then let it drop back to her side.

"Wait there a second while I come around," Lucas told Teal.

He bounded out of the driver's-side door and was around to her side before she had a chance to open her own door. Jerking the passenger door open, Lucas reached in and tenderly lifted her in his arms.

"Hey. I can walk on my own. I'm not that hurt."

Before she could blink, he'd carried her through the

front door and gently lowered her onto an overstuffed sofa. The room around her looked worn and slightly shabby, but it was cozy and inviting and smelled heavenly.

Lucas said something to the old woman in Navajo. Teal had been studying the language, but the only words she recognized were *ya'at'eeh* and *amá sání—hello* and *grandmother*.

In English, he introduced them. "Special Agent Teal Benaly, this is my grandmother, Helena Gray Goats." He leaned down close to Teal's ear and whispered. "When you speak to her, call her *Grandmother*."

"You are in much pain, Daughter." The old woman bent over her and spoke in a rusty voice. "Before my medicine can help, you must have a short blessing ceremony to restore harmony. My grandson will do the Sing as I prepare the elixir."

She reached into her pocket and handed something to Teal. "Here's a fetish to hold. It has guided the women of my clan for generations. It will see you through."

Looking down at her palm, Teal saw the crude statue of a woman that seemed to be made from a combination of turquoise and white shell. Tipping her chin up again, she looked closely at the kindly grandmother; Helena Gray Goats certainly seemed more spry than Teal.

Teal took a good look at her. The old face was round and plump but crisscrossed with a zillion deep crevices, making her look as if she had lived through at least eighty summer suns. Her expression was friendly and pleasant, and the sweet face was framed by thin wisps of silver hair.

Looking up into the woman's kind, concerned eyes, Teal was stunned to realize that one of the old lady's eyes was black and the other blue. Even though she felt no fear from Lucas's grandmother, a chill ran down her spine simply at the sight of those odd eyes.

The old woman patted the backside of Teal's closed fist, then glanced up at her grandson. "Do what you can, but be quick."

The elderly lady turned, and Teal watched her hunched-over body as she made her way past an elaborate Navajo blanket hung in front of an interior doorway. When she'd disappeared, Lucas sat beside Teal on the sofa.

"Grandmother must be nearing ninety," he told her in a quiet voice. "Osteoporosis and rheumatism wrack her body, yet the elixir she makes keeps her walking and taking care of herself. She'll be able to cure your aches."

"What's this about a curing ceremony you are supposed to sing for me?"

He smiled and a flicker of some special emotion appeared in his eyes. "Medicine men are trained to do curing ceremonies for the People. Each ceremony is called a Sing because a big part of it includes chanting. But the ceremonies also include special potions, and occasionally there are sacred sand paintings that must be done.

"Most of our Sings take days, and can be over a week long," he explained. "The whole point of them is to restore balance and harmony to the patient. I have a short chant I will perform for you now, if I may. But a Sing can only help those who understand and believe. I'm not sure…"

"Just do it, will you? I don't wanna have to tell your *amá sání* that her grandson refused to help."

An hour later, Lucas had stepped outside and Teal was seated at a table in a fascinating, old-style kitchen, located behind the Navajo blanket she'd seen from the front room. She was watching Lucas's grandmother as she bustled around gathering dried leaves from bundles of herbs that hung from the ceiling. A little strange-seeming to Teal's city girl's eyes, but she figured this room had to be the origin of those mouthwatering smells. Yum.

Lucas's Sing had been quite interesting, mostly because he had a wonderful mellow singing voice. Teal hadn't understood a word, of course, and she had no idea why he'd done things like throwing little flecks of pollen in the air. But his tone and his touch had soothed her, calmed her. It had been an experience she would never forget.

"You must wear this," his grandmother told her as she placed a heavy Navajo rug over her head and draped it across her shoulders.

"I love these blankets," Teal gushed. "Each of them looks different. Do artists like Lucas make them?"

The old woman shook her head. "Dineh weaving is done only by women. For some of us it is a calling, passed down through the generations from mother to daughter. We were originally taught by Spider Woman and we weave today out of respect for her.

"The rugs you see in this hogan are old, woven by my clan. Some by me in younger days."

"Really? They're beautiful. You're very talented." Teal noticed three big pots steaming on the wood-burning stove. "What smells so good in here?"

Lucas's grandmother turned to the stove. "This is for you." She picked up one of the pots by its handle and placed the whole thing on a large wooden plate sitting on the table directly in front of Teal.

"You breathe the steam," the old woman said as she gently bent Teal's head over the pot.

Ah. Like one of those old vaporizers people used on kids to help their breathing. Teal vaguely remembered her sister needing one as a baby.

As she took deep breaths of the slightly sweet and spicy steam, Teal could feel her body relaxing even more. Her shoulders dropped and her eyelids grew heavy. For the first time in almost two days, the aching began to subside.

A few minutes later, Lucas's grandmother removed the steaming pot and placed a bowl of something that looked like thick soup before her. "You eat. I will sit. We talk."

"What is this—stew?" Whatever it was, the stuff was giving off that heavenly smell.

"It is known as mutton stew. It is made from lamb meat."

Teal put a spoonful in her mouth and moaned in pleasure. It was to die for.

"You eat," Grandmother insisted as she sat down beside her. "I want to tell you a story."

"Hmm," Teal managed past her full mouth. Anything the elderly woman said was okay by her right now.

"There once was a boy, a bright child with many talents. He laughed and ran and dreamed in the sun." The old woman watched her closely, making sure Teal was paying attention.

She was definitely paying attention, and felt sure the story would turn out to be about Lucas. Filling her mouth again, she nodded for his grandmother to continue.

"This young boy was bright and had inherited special gifts from his maternal clan, gifts his grandmother would help him to understand.

"The more he learned and understood, the more unhappy his parents became. Because, you see, they did not possess the gifts. His special gifts had skipped the mother and were passed down to him instead."

Teal stopped eating for a moment. "His own mother was jealous of the gift he'd inherited from her family?"

Ignoring the question, Grandmother continued, "As he grew, loneliness became his constant companion. Cousins and playmates teased and made fun. So the boy stopped playing and practiced running faster—and dreamed more and more."

Teal didn't like the way this story was going. She set the spoon down and watched the elder's expression. The unusual old eyes were watery with unspent emotion. Suddenly Teal's appetite disappeared.

"The day he mastered his gift and saw the future

was his worst day. He saw his own life—alone through the years, save for his grandmother.

"You see, Daughter," Grandmother continued in a raspy, quiet voice. "The boy's parents could not bear their son's differences. That very day they left the sacred lands, never to return. They turned their backs on their clan and on their only son."

With her stomach churning, Teal brushed away a single tear that escaped to run down her cheek. "How old was he then?"

"He'd celebrated his eleventh year only weeks before."

*Oh, Lucas.*

Teal's own life had changed dramatically when she was eleven, so she immediately felt empathy for the sad little boy he must've been. When they'd first met, she'd believed they didn't have much in common except being loners. But now she knew they were alike in other ways, as well. Her heart cried for him.

*Oh, Lucas…*

## Chapter 6

Under the cobalt-blue sky, Lucas had been pacing behind his grandmother's hogan and worrying about Teal for several hours now. He knew she would be safe with his *amá sání*, but would her Anglo sensibilities allow her Navajo side to accept their help?

She simply had to take the assistance his grandmother offered. He wasn't sure he could stand another minute of watching the pain reflected in Teal's eyes as her body fought her spirit.

For lack of anything better to do with his hands, he picked up a rock and prepared to skip it across his grandmother's stock tank. Before he could follow through, the Brotherhood's satellite phone buzzed in his pocket.

The specialized ring told him it was his cousin,

Michael Ayze, calling. A founding member of the Brotherhood, Michael was also Councilman Ayze's eldest son. And he'd been the key to Lucas convincing the FBI that he should be Teal's translator and guide.

"*Ya'at'eeh,* Cousin." Michael's voice came through the earpiece. "Have you heard the news?"

Lucas remembered Kody telling him that his brother Hunter Long and Michael Ayze had recently taken leave from their jobs in order to scour the northern sections of the reservation, looking for a lost map. Perhaps this news would be good for a change.

"News?" He waited for Michael to explain.

"You haven't been listening to the radio this afternoon?" Michael asked, surprising him by the different direction. "The Dineh station, KTNN…660?"

Impatient for his cousin to get to the point, Lucas's breath caught when he became fully aware that for the first time in his memory he wasn't reading Michael's thoughts. He couldn't foresee his cousin's words.

Lucas's silence was apparently a good enough answer to the question for Michael.

"The news is not good, I'm afraid," Michael told him. "You know that DJ, Chili Redhorse? The one who likes to stir up political trouble? Well, his most recent rant has been about the wasting of our water resources by the coal company at Black Mesa mines.

"This morning," Michael continued, "he informed his listeners that a decent, hardworking Navajo had been murdered for investigating the trouble near the mines. Then Chili went on to say that the feds have put a brand-new agent on the case, a woman called Special Agent Teal Benaly."

"What? How did he hear about her? I thought this was a *nonpublic* joint investigation."

"Not anymore. I thought you should know."

Lucas was stunned and afraid for Teal's safety. Whoever had murdered the one who'd died now knew exactly who was looking for him. That could not be good.

He hung up the phone and tried to calm down. Looking toward the skies, expecting to spot his friends, the Bird People, Lucas grew even more concerned when he realized how quiet it had suddenly become in the skies and piñon forests surrounding his grandmother's hogan.

Where were the Bird People? Had they abandoned him, too, now that he could no longer read others' thoughts?

And more to the point, was this unearthly quiet somehow related to the Skinwalkers? A shudder of foreboding ran up his spine as he dashed back to his grandmother's hogan to check on Teal.

Lucas wrapped Teal's sleeping form in the blanket that had been covering her as she dozed at the kitchen table. Then he lifted her into his arms.

"Did you give her a sleeping potion, *Amá sání?* That isn't part of the cure."

His grandmother smiled at him. "I know this cure better than you, Grandson. Her body needs rest. She has had the elixir. But for it to work, she must sleep. The longer, the better."

Frowning, Lucas shook his head at the wily old lady. "Now she can't even go to her own home tonight. It may be dangerous and I couldn't leave her passed out and alone. So the only choice is my place.

"That's what you had in mind, wasn't it?" he added, catching the twinkle in his grandmother's eyes.

"She will be safe with you. I have seen her future."

"Yeah? Well, I don't want to hear about it." He stormed out of the hogan with Teal in his arms.

Not daring to listen to his grandmother's prognostications about Teal's future in case it was something he didn't want to know, Lucas set his jaw and walked away from the possibilities. The beautiful special agent would damn sure be safe with him.

Trying to be as gentle as possible, he tucked her prone body into the second seat of his SUV and steadied her with more blankets to keep her from rolling off. His house was only a half mile away. But he sure wished Teal had been awake enough to consent to spending the night there.

Lucas didn't like the idea of her waking up in a strange place and not knowing how she got there. And he seriously doubted that Teal was going to like the idea all that well, either—once she woke up and thought about it.

As he drove up the hill past his grandmother's meadow, he tried listening to his own spirit instead of the empty spaces where others' futures and feelings used to reside. But all he could think about was the sleeping special agent.

This uncommon woman was so much more than the slash of erotic heat that had always seared him in his dreams. Whenever he was around her, the nearness still set off electric sparks between them. But now that he'd talked to her, gotten closer to her and knew about her energy and empathy, his feelings for her seemed deeper, stronger.

She was sensual, with those big ebony eyes and long, silky hair—yes. Sensual and immensely touchable. But he now knew some of the other reasons why her spirit had called out to him across time and space.

There was an aura of destiny surrounding the two of them. Though he still could not hear or see the future, his instincts were screaming at him to stay close to her. They must've been meant to come together for some purpose.

As he pulled into the yard in front of his studio, Lucas looked up at the indigo skies and the first sparkle of evening stars. Wherever their destinies would lead them, he would protect her with his life.

He had no choice.

Teal knew she was dreaming. She'd even had this dream before, though she'd tried not to. It always started out the same pleasant way.

*A brilliant summer sun glittered across the expanse of water, shooting sparkly fireworks to glare back into her eyes. It was a wonderfully warm and lazy day. Perfect for a special time with father and daughter together.*

*Teal always loved coming here for vacation at her aunt's house on the reservation. There were cousins to play with and neat things like swimming and fishing to do.*

*But the best part was getting time alone with her father. He worked so hard all year and there was never enough time for them to be together.*

*This year was even better than summers before. Mommy and Christie had stayed home so Christie could go to day camp with her friends. Daddy was all Teal's for once.*

*And he wasn't still mad at her for refusing to wear that bulky old life vest. After all, Daddy didn't wear one. Besides that, she was a big girl—almost a teen-ager and almost knew how to swim.*

*He'd even said he would let her bait her own hook this trip. A tiny tickle of anticipation ran through her fingers when she thought of hooking one of those squiggly worms on the hook the way Daddy had taught her. But she wanted him to be proud of her. So she chewed her bottom lip and waited for him to finish putting down the anchor.*

*Daddy turned and smiled at her. Then he handed her the special rod he'd rigged up just for her.*

*This was going to be the best day ever.*

The dream suddenly changed, twisted and became a nightmare. It always did this same thing at this same point. Just like an old familiar horror movie. It turned from feel-good to terrifying in one instant.

But this time, instead of the choking panic of being about to drown and then the terrible guilt that always followed, Teal's nightmare went in a different direction.

*Following close. Chasing her. She knew the demon was right behind and she pushed her muscles to swim faster. Get away.*

*Then all of a sudden there were dreadful images in the water right ahead. Yellow staring eyes. Red blood dripping from sharp, disembodied fangs and spreading through the murkiness toward her.*

Teal tried to wake herself up. This was just a dream. But the more she tried, the closer the red bloom came to closing in around her. Not a dream, but definitely not any reality that she recognized.

Holy crap! She was going to die. From a damned dream.

*Just then, a hand came down on her shoulder and scared her even more, until she turned and saw the dark form, a shadow of a man, reaching out to enclose her in his arms. There was no fear coming from the solid form who'd arrived to save her.*

*Daddy? Had her father's spirit returned to make the evil go away?*

"Teal, take it easy. Come on, Bright Eyes. It's only a bad dream. Wake up."

The calm steady voice finally got through to her. Lucas. She let him pull her up and enfold her against his chest. Balanced tenuously between nightmare and reality, Teal collapsed into his arms.

"The eyes. So creepy. They were the biggest ugliest yellow eyes imaginable."

"Don't think about them," he whispered as he began to rock her like a child. "You're safe with me."

At those words, her trembling subsided. She did feel

safe. Protected. She could feel the steady beating of his heart under her ear. Nothing could reach her here.

He rubbed her back, then bent to place a kiss against her temple. "You're okay. Safe," he mumbled over and over.

The horrible dream began to drift away like a whisper of smoke in a strong wind. "I'm safe here with you," she mumbled.

But in the next instant it hit her. Where was *here?*

She lifted her chin to look around. The dawn was bringing light into wherever she was. But shadows still clung to the farthest corners, and light was puddling in tiny pools near towering windows.

Glancing up she found soaring ceilings, with skylights and wooden beams. This certainly wasn't Lucas's grandmother's house.

Teal started to feel uncomfortable. Turning around, she gazed into Lucas's sexy sensitive eyes as he studied her. "What place is this?"

He tenderly rubbed his knuckles along her jawline. "You're in my studio. My home."

In a deliberate and slow move, she pushed his hand from her face. "Why am I at your house? The last thing I remember was being in the kitchen and drinking some of your grandmother's herb tea."

Lots of strange emotions flitted across his face at once. They told her most of what she needed to know.

She shoved hard against his arms and frowned. "What happened? Did that nice little old grandmother of yours dope me?"

His brow quirked. "Drugs? Hardly. But you needed

rest in order for your body to heal, so she gave you a sleeping potion. How do you feel?"

"Cripes. Sleeping pills in herb tea." She narrowed her eyes and sat straight up in bed. Bed?

Meaning to push past him to climb off whatever this was, Teal tried to body-block him with her upper torso. But Lucas held her down.

"Hold on," he told her quietly. "Take it easy until you have a chance to get your legs under you. How are the pains this morning?" His voice was low and sweet, but she tried to brush aside the hypnotic quality of it.

Ignoring his question, she checked the area below them and discovered they were not sitting on a bed but on a long suede sofa. That calmed her a bit, but she still had a lot of questions.

"Why did you bring me here to your house? If we had to leave your grandmother's, why didn't you just drive me home?"

"There were reasons. We can talk about it after you tell me how you're feeling. Focus, Bright Eyes."

*Focus?* The dreamy, out-of-this-world sensitive was telling *her* to focus?

"I am absolutely fine, thank you very much," she said with perfect enunciation. "But you'd better start giving me some answers pretty damn quick. Or my next question will be why shouldn't I arrest you for kidnapping?"

"Are you really okay? You're sure there're no aches left?"

His incessant questioning finally made her stop and take inventory of her body. How *was* she feeling? The answer echoed back to her across a cavernous empty stomach. Hungry.

But not in pain. She turned her arms over to check the bruises, but they had faded to nothing. No aching left at all. Interesting.

Slanting a glance in his direction, she was stopped cold as she got a good look at his expression. The way he was staring at her, with a combination of concern and sensual desperation, made her belly jump. She'd lost her focus again. Her hunger for food turned into something much more dangerous to her well-being.

Those languid, half-lidded, dreamy eyes were calling out to her in a strangely familiar manner. As if she'd seen them countless times. And not only did it feel as if she'd seen them before—even knew them intimately—it was as if she'd lost herself more than once to their draw.

She had never in her life felt anything quite like this, but she was positive she'd made love with the near stranger sitting beside her—somewhere. Some time.

Lucas watched while the expressions on her face went from fear to anger and now to something much more compelling and dangerous. Her lids were blinking furiously as she tilted her head. It made her look vulnerable, even a little fragile.

His Teal—fragile? No way.

Deciding to make her snap out of it, he lowered his mouth to her ear. "Don't look at me that way, Special Agent love. Not unless you mean to hold me off with your gun."

He held her gaze and watched timidity turn to heat.

Uncertainty turned to a come-hither look. An urgent bolt of raw need ripped into his gut, leaving him nearly helpless.

It was too much for this all-too-human man. Grasping her chin, he dipped his head and canted a kiss across that quirky mouth. The kiss shocked his sensibilities, so he took a quick nip at her bottom lip and then backed off.

It was not a particularly satisfying kiss to his mind, it had been over much too quickly. But he'd been afraid to push her. He would rather wait and do the job right another time.

But still, the mere touching of their lips had caused his stomach to flip as though he'd taken a punch to the gut. It left him slightly light-headed and breathing heavily.

He searched her face for answers to what had just happened between them. A simple touch of lips, nothing more, had created such havoc zinging through his veins.

But what he saw in her face undid whatever reserve and resolve he might've had. At first, her expression simply mirrored his surprise. Not so much surprise at his actions, he knew, but at her own reaction to them.

Then her pupils darkened and grew wide. He stood close and felt a tremor run through her body. She licked her lips and cleared her throat.

The expression on her face said what no words could tell him. He'd seen it in his dreams far too often. She wanted him. Now. With a desperation that matched his own.

But in reality, they had met just a couple of days ago. How could he satisfy their hunger now without ruining whatever chance he had of protecting her?

There was no mistaking the look in her eyes, however.

"Didn't you...?" he began with a raspy, hoarse voice. "I mean, I thought you wanted an answer to why you couldn't go home last night? I thought..."

"That was *so* five minutes ago," she mumbled, surprising even herself. But Teal wasn't surprised enough to stop and actually think things through. She placed both her palms against the sides of his head and dragged him down for another kiss.

This time, their lips met in a way not nearly as gentle nor as shockingly scary as the last time. This time, the kiss was all tongue and moans and desperation from both of them.

The sensation of wanting something she'd known existed but had never experienced shot through Teal, rattling her senses and scattering what was left of her brain. What was so different about this man? Had she known him before?

No. Every kiss she'd ever experienced before this was nothing. *Nada.* Zip—compared to his. What's more, every previous lover, every "I want you" from the past didn't mean a damned thing to her now. Not since she'd experienced *this* man's kiss.

Lucas wrapped an arm around her and tugged her roughly to his chest. The new position made her nipples brush against the inside of her sweatshirt, creating incredible friction and driving her wild. She felt the tender peaks harden and tighten.

Barely able to breathe, she didn't care, wanting only more of those narcotic kisses. Nothing else seemed to matter.

Lucas pulled back slightly to make sure she was still okay. Her eyes were wide open and studying him, while her tongue slipped out and licked her swollen bottom lip. But she didn't look unhappy. She looked like a woman who was in a sensual trance. It worried him for a second, wondering if she knew what she was doing—what *they* were doing.

He glanced down her body and watched the tips of her breasts react to his gaze. They peaked and lifted, as if begging for his touch.

His throat felt dry and a drop of sweat trickled down his temple. All he could think of at the moment was putting his mouth on the luscious curve of her breasts. Things between them seemed suddenly out of his control.

"Bright Eyes." It was all he could manage as she reached for the hem of her sweatshirt and lifted it up and over her head in one swift maneuver.

That moved him past all talking as he stared at her lovely nakedness. She hadn't worn a bra and he'd never been so glad of anything in his whole life.

Perfect. Like a classic work of art, she was perfect. Small and full. Rounded and exquisitely formed. An exact fit for the palms of his hands.

His mouth watered and his fingers itched to touch.

But he shouldn't. After all, he *knew* her. But she didn't know him in return.

"Teal, are you still wrapped up in that bad dream? Do you know what…"

"Be quiet," she said as she picked up his hands and placed them against her straining nipples. "I know what I want."

Ah, hell. His heart was thundering so loudly in his throat that he almost missed her soft moans. His hands automatically began to caress and massage her breasts.

He had dreamed of her a thousand times. But a thousand times had not prepared him for the reality of Teal.

Her hands went to his head, drilled into his hair as she pulled his face down to her chest. He gave up and let his mouth replace a hand. Swirling his tongue over one tight nub, he brushed a calloused thumb over the other one. Her heart began thundering in time with his own.

She tasted sweet and salty and as arousing as hell. In another minute he would be unable to stop. He knew what would happen then the way he knew his own dreams.

But he couldn't. *They shouldn't.* Did she even know how close he was?

He wrapped an arm around her waist and dragged both of them up on their feet. Filling a hand with her firm bottom, he pressed his hard arousal against the juncture of her thighs. Trying to shock her.

Still, his own libido refused to let him stop entirely. He was nearly bent in two so he could keep laving and tugging at her nipples, first one then the other. He'd wanted her to call a halt to things, but he was only half-convinced himself that they could stop now.

So he was only half-crazy? Was it in a dream that he heard her ragged breathing and noticed she was reaching between them for his zipper? Or was it absolute reality?

The shock of her warm hand against his groin as she worked to undo the button on his jeans finally brought him around. He broke off and pulled away from her fingers.

"Teal, I still don't think now is the right…"

Their gazes met—locked. Her big ebony eyes filled with tears, and he couldn't guess why. Had she wanted them to stop—or to go on?

The answer came loud and clear when right before his eyes the reality undid her own jeans and stepped out of both them and her panties. Standing naked before him, she had tears welling in her eyes and a look of lonely desolation on that beautiful face. Teal tentatively reached a hand out to him in a pleading gesture.

Lucas groaned and took her by the shoulders, crushing her against him once more. He placed a kiss of quiet desperation against her neck, and almost forgot for the time being that he wasn't crazy.

"It's okay, Bright Eyes," he whispered. "Whatever you want."

Holding her, he let his hands roam over her naked body.

*Remembering the dream. Relearning her present. Discovering new realities.*

# *Chapter 7*

In Lucas's mind's eye, he could visualize what he wanted to do. What he had already done with her—to her—*for* her in his dreams.

But the reality was so much better now that they had actually met. There was something powerful about pleasuring a strong woman. About feeling that power as she surrendered to her own needs. It turned him on as never before.

With his heart knocking against his rib cage, he slipped his fingers down through the curls between her thighs. She whimpered, but it sounded more like a feral growl as she opened her legs and invited him in.

He was trembling as badly as she was, but not enough to stop. So he dropped to his knees between her legs and used his free hand to band around her bottom, holding her close and tight.

He was shocked by what two supposed strangers were doing, and gratified it was even better than he had dreamed. Not too shocked to slide a finger into the depths of her, however, he tested her wetness and probed the dark places he'd experienced in his dreams so many times.

Moaning, she squirmed in his arms and began to pant. He let the tip of his middle finger dance across her internal muscles and felt them quivering in response. Her panting became stronger, with a much higher pitch.

His tongue actually itched, desperate to taste her feminine wetness. He shot a glance up her torso and found Teal's eyes closed and her body swaying. Tightening his grip, he pulled his fingers from within her and replaced them with his mouth.

She squealed and jerked when his tongue made contact with her most tender of places. But he continued to hold her close, determined to wring every passionate moan and cry from deep inside her before he let her go.

Lucas's own body was pleading with him for release. It had been a long time since he had made love to a woman—in real life. But this wasn't about him. It was all about giving Teal what she wanted.

"Mmm. Hot silk," he mumbled as he licked and laved. "Perfect."

Swirling his tongue in ever-tightening circles, Lucas knew when her moans grew desperate and the muscles under his lips began to quake. She gasped, dug her fingers into his scalp and screamed an obscenity.

He drank of her sweetness, and fought to hold her up as her body became weak and boneless. In the end, letting her collapse back on the sofa, Lucas couldn't stop his satisfied smile—even as his own body was pounding and screaming for release.

"Oh. Oh. Oh," she gasped.

He watched as she tried to shake off the remnants of her desire so she could look at him. How beautiful she was, with her face and chest flushed in that sexy rosy glow. And with her long ebony hair, normally up in a bun or back in a thick braid, all tossed and streaming across her back and breasts in a perfect sensual disaster.

Lucas had never seen anything so fantastic.

Suddenly she jumped up, looked around the floor and found her jeans. He thought reality must have crashed in on them. Their daylight dream would be over now for sure.

But he was beyond confused when she didn't scurry to pull the pants on. Instead, she frantically dug into the pockets, looking for something.

"Damn it. These aren't the right ones," she cried.

Turning to him, she had the strangest expression on her face. "I...I'm sorry."

He took the two steps closer to be ready for dragging her into his arms. "Sorry? For what? You're perfect."

She half-heartedly pushed at his shoulders and held up the jeans for his inspection. "I could've sworn I stuck a condom into the little watch pocket of these jeans. But it's not there. Must've been the pair I didn't wash."

"A what?" Had she really just said what he thought she'd said?

At least she had the grace to look slightly embarrassed. "You know. *Protection*," she said in a stage whisper. "It would be only fair. I mean, you didn't. Uh. You haven't…"

She looked so willing. And he was sorely tempted. *No way.*

"*Protection* is my worry, Bright Eyes. And right now, it's not a problem." He skimmed a stray piece of hair back off her face and hooked it behind her ear.

Her eyes narrowed as she glanced down his body to the truth of his problem. She brushed her hand lightly against his tight arousal, at the moment barely contained behind the zipper of his jeans.

"No problem, huh?" she said with a wry smile.

For a second he couldn't say a word. Then he took a big breath. Shifted his own jeans, trying to find some room. And finally lifted her hand away.

Holding her by the wrist, he shook his head. "Later, Special Agent love. It looks to me like you're feeling just a little bit too fine this morning. I think we'd better get you back to work after we make you something to eat.

"We can finish our other kind of…work another time."

The sexy dream girl turned back into the FBI Special Agent right before his eyes as she jerked her jeans up over her hips and scowled at him. It was what he knew must be for the best. But still...

*Ah, hell.*

She was in major trouble here.

Muttering to herself about jocks who were so full of themselves that a mere woman could not be the protection provider for once, Teal jammed her running shoes onto her feet and ignored the socks. Apparently, good-looking Mister "I'm-the-Protector" here had slipped both her shoes and socks off when he'd laid her down on the sofa last night. Good damn thing he hadn't removed anything else while she was drugged.

What had gotten into her, jumping the guy like that? There would be no chalking it up to hypnotism or a date-rape drug.

Actually, Teal had to admit she'd known this very thing would happen yesterday when she'd stopped and bought a box of condoms and then hidden one in a pair of jeans. But for her to actually attack the man and let him *know* she'd wanted much more even if he didn't— Well, that was just beyond stupid.

Having sex with a stranger, a Navajo sensitive stranger who won Iron Man competitions at that, was so *not* in her job description.

But, oh, what that particular stranger could do to her with his hands and his mouth! Man, when had being bad ever felt so good?

Shaking her head, she tried focusing well enough to follow him through his studio and into a galley kitchen that connected the studio to the house. Teal thought about how much she loved her job. It had taken the place of friends and family after she'd left home. The Bureau had become her everything.

She simply could not let *any* man distract her and ruin it. Her world needed to get back to being black and white. These gray areas were killing her.

By the time she sat down at the kitchen table and looked up to find him, Lucas was already starting the coffeemaker. "I know you're hungry, what can I get you? Eggs? Muesli and yogurt? Fruit?"

"Muesli and yogurt? Eeeww. Health food. Don't you have anything greasy or sweet? Bacon? Donuts? I need to get a headstart on my daily ration of fat and sugar."

He'd had his back turned to her, but she heard him chuckling before he said anything. "Afraid I don't have any of that junk, Bright Eyes. You'll have to settle for nongreasy scrambled eggs and a sweet fresh apple."

Turning, his face became the picture of sobriety. "But while you wait, here's a jump on your caffeine intake for the day."

She accepted the cup of coffee and tried not to check out the front of his jeans. Was he still wanting her? She knew for a fact he'd been in need just a few minutes ago. Would he have conquered it by now? By now she'd managed to get past her own needs. Honestly she had.

A few moments later Lucas sat down beside her and they both dug into a platter of eggs. She marveled at how good a cook he was. Had he learned as something

to do in his loneliness? she wondered. Teal was a
terrible cook, so she didn't bother with it. Not when
the local That's-a-Burger made such great breakfast
sandwiches and hamburgers.

As her hunger subsided, her curiosity about the man
she had just attacked grew. "Could you tell me more
about this mind-reading trick you supposedly can do?
For instance, are you reading my mind right now?"

Nothing like jumping right into the deep end, she
chided herself. There were several other questions she
could've asked. But nooo.

Lucas stared down at his half-empty coffee cup for
a few long seconds. She nearly opened her mouth and
asked something else to get him off the hook. Damn,
what would her interrogation instructor back at
Quantico have to say about that?

Finally, he lifted his head. "Actually, no. I can't
read your mind at all anymore. I seem to have lost the
ability."

"When did that happen?"

"Sometime yesterday."

"Yesterday? Have you got any idea what changed?"
Teal was beginning to think Lucas had finally figured
out that he couldn't fool her with magic tricks. So he'd
probably decided to tell her that his special powers had
suddenly disappeared. Smart guy.

He looked over at her and took another minute
before answering. Meanwhile, the expression in his
eyes was a stunner. A combination of hurt, along with
desolation and need were laid bare right there for her
to see.

An arrow of comradeship drove through her heart. She had felt all those things, too. For most of her life. But she always tried her damnedest not to let them show.

Feeling pity for him and remorse for herself, she was suddenly very sorry she'd jumped the man before they'd had a chance to get to know one another better. Why had she done that anyway? Okay, so he was gorgeous and sexy. All lean torso and muscled arms, and with those gooey chestnut eyes. But she'd met sexy strangers before and nothing like that had ever happened between them.

While he swallowed one last gulp of cold coffee and cleared his throat, she tried to figure out her motivations.

"I don't really understand what changed," he began at last. "I've always hated being odd. But in Navajo tradition, balance and harmony and accepting what can't be changed is the way we try to live our lives. So hatred for my own 'gift' went against tradition—and I hated myself for that, too.

"Still," he continued with a deep sigh. "I've wished a million times for the gift to go away. And now that it has, I've found myself wishing for a way to make it come back. I hate the change."

*Oh, Lucas.*

In the back of her brain, Teal was beginning to understand why she had made a move on him this morning. They were a lot alike. Somehow, they had two similar spirits. She'd already known who and what he was—because he was the male version of her lonely self. He wasn't a stranger.

But he looked so forlorn, so miserable, that she decided to try another shot at becoming his friend. "You know the coolest thing about being an FBI agent? It's an ever-changing experience. I had to get used to that in the beginning because I thought I hated change, too.

"Now I just love getting to carry a gun and looking tough. *And* being able to call for backup when things turn too scary."

Lucas studied her for a moment and then a light of recognition stirred deep within his eyes. "Everything is so scattered and distant on this reservation. Out here, backup is nearly always an hour away."

Teal let herself give him a real smile, one meant to say more than mere words. "I've come to understand the distances, yes. That's why I've decided to be happy you and I are going to be riding together."

She reached over and laid her hand on his in a true companion gesture. "We can be each other's backup, don't you think? Maybe my gut instincts about people will help compensate for your loss. I've honed my abilities to read people by more than what they say. It's a great tool for any lawman to have and I'll share it with you."

His eyes were doing that gooey thing again as he looked at her in silence.

"It's a deal, Special Agent love," he finally told her. "I'd be proud to watch your back—or any other body part that you care to name."

She jerked her hand away. "Fine. Let's get going then. There's *work* waiting for us, partner."

* * *

Not far away, the Skinwalker soldier known as the Burrowing Owl deliberately moved at a slow pace down the outside steps of his day job toward the parking lot. He wasn't in his Skinwalker persona at the moment and had to walk, not fly. But he had just found a substitute to take his day job for now, so he could change over and go back to fulfilling his promises to the Navajo Wolf.

He'd heard the radio program this morning, naming that new Brotherhood female interest, the FBI agent, as the lead investigator on the murder case. It had given him a great idea.

If the Wolf's purpose was to confuse the Brotherhood and keep them busy, this new development presented a perfect opportunity. The Burrowing Owl had researched a few ideas for making that agent believe her life was being threatened—using the type of weapons that a normal human murderer would think of, not a Skinwalker.

Worrying about her life ought to make at least those two Brotherhood soldiers he'd seen with her the other night in Many Caves Canyon forget about the Skinwalkers for a while. And maybe if he was real smart, the Owl figured he could find ways to involve more Brotherhood warriors, too.

Pleased with himself for being so brilliant, the Owl snuck into the stand of ponderosa pines that grew on the far side of the parking lot. He was also determined to find a way to outsmart those damned birds that were always getting in his way. Maybe later.

For now, he just needed a moment's privacy in order to say the chants that would change him over to the Dineh's traditional symbol of death and disaster. The Skinwalker Burrowing Owl.

It had taken quite a while for Lucas to get them back on the road that morning as he'd had to introduce Snow to Teal. Then he'd needed to feed the spoiled *bilagaana* cat his morning canned sardines and kibble while Teal made several calls to her field office.

And lastly, he'd wanted to show Teal around his studio. There hadn't been time for him to describe all the kinds of traditional Navajo arts that he was known for. He'd briefly pointed out examples of the mud pottery, the turquoise and silver jewelry and the sand paintings. But the tradition and history of sand painting alone would've taken hours to explain.

At long last they were in his SUV and on the way to her house. She'd wanted to go home to change and dig out some more of her notes. He was okay with that, because he'd wanted to make sure she rested for the rest of today. Looking drawn and exhausted again, she needed more time and her boss said she could take as much time as she needed.

He'd been an ass this morning to let her get to him the way she had. But the fragile seeds of possibilities he'd found in her eyes had made him temporarily lose his mind.

He hadn't been quite sure of the extent of those

possibilities. Would she really be able to accept someone like him? Was her obvious need for him only temporary? He'd lost himself in the opportunity.

What a jerk. He should've been thinking of what was best for her. She'd almost lost her life sliding down the mountain less than thirty-six hours ago. Maybe her needs had been a remnant of a self-preservation adrenaline rush.

Shaking the cobwebs out of his brain, Lucas vowed to make things between them stay much more lighthearted from now on. He knew about their connection. She did not.

"Do you have any plans formulated on how to go about your murder investigation?" he asked in an effort to steer them both to considering the business at hand.

"Not really. I've decided to count on you to help me understand the problems at the mine. And maybe together we can pinpoint which Navajos would have the best motives to have that covert investigator murdered."

"I'll tell you whatever I can. But Navajos don't *plan* to kill people like white men do. Navajos do kill each other once in awhile, but generally it's because someone got drunk or accidentally kills someone in a bar fight. Accidents, even a surprise attack of rage on rare occasions, do happen and people get killed. But for a Navajo to scheme to kill for profit or for protection is unthinkable."

"Really? I hadn't heard that. Why?"

How to explain so that she would understand? Lucas considered the many ways of beginning the story and opted for a short, black-and-white version for her benefit.

"Traditional Navajos do not believe that people have a soul that will go on without them after death," he began. "Death is just death, not a beginning. But the Dineh do believe that if you are out of harmony before you die and don't have a chance to get back into balance, your bad spirit will be stuck roaming the earth long after you are dead."

He slanted a look at Teal and she was nodding thoughtfully. Good. He'd apparently picked a good place to begin.

"A Navajo man who plans to kill," he went on, "is just asking for the bad part of his spirit to be stuck forever."

"I see. So we should be looking for a modern Navajo—or maybe a white person living on the rez?"

"It's not quite that simple. There does happen to be one group of traditional Navajos who make an appearance in every generation and who give up on the true Way, usually for profit or power. They take up forbidden things that are the exact opposite of what the rest of us believe. Things we consider taboo and witchcraft."

"Witchcraft? Not really?"

"Don't make fun, Bright Eyes. You might be sorry to have ignored the possibilities."

"You're wrong about me. I would never consider making fun of witchcraft. I even studied voodoo and witch cults and their legal ramifications in one of my college law-enforcement classes. Nasty stuff."

Well, that went better than he could've hoped. "Yes, it is. Our witches are worse than the run-of-the-mill, though. Because ours are such a departure from the Navajo Way. The People have named our witches Skinwalkers. But you shouldn't mention that word too loudly. People will figure you're a witch in disguise and will refuse to deal with you."

"Skinwalkers! Even the name sounds dangerous. What's its meaning?"

"Just as it suggests. A Skinwalker is a witch who does many bad things. But the worst is his being able to change himself over into an animal with superhuman powers."

"Doesn't sound good. And I suppose these Skinwalkers don't mind killing people for fun and profit?"

"That's right." He took a second and thought about her complete acceptance of such an odd idea. Seemed too easy.

"You're not buying the shape-shifting part, are you?"

"Yes, I am," she said with complete equanimity. "I understand that susceptible people will accept any concept as long as it's fed to them the right way and for a long enough period. And when people accept and believe, then it doesn't really matter whether the concept is absolute fact or not. The damage can be just as deadly."

Well, what do you know about that? The woman was as intelligent as she looked. Must be her Navajo heritage.

Lucas just hoped she would never have to face the reality of this one particular deadly concept.

"Go. I'll be fine." Teal was trying to shove Lucas out of her front door. "We've checked the place. No intruders to be found. I'll rest today and won't work. I swear. We'll start again tomorrow, but you don't need to hang around and watch me take naps today."

"Are you sure? Maybe I should wait outside in my SUV. Just in case you need anything."

"No." She gave him another little push. "Don't waste your time. I'm going to take a shower. Go home. Be creative."

As she locked the door behind him and turned toward the bathroom, Teal found herself smiling. She wasn't entirely sure when it had happened, but sometime during their car trip back to her house they had become friends. Apparently, being almost lovers first hadn't ruined their fledgling relationship.

She'd also come to another interesting conclusion. Lucas must've convinced himself as a young boy that he could truly read minds. No child would've deliberately put up with being as isolated as he'd claimed to be.

Teal thought back to her own childhood for a moment and shook her head. Hers was goofy, not really isolated, yet not really Miss Popularity, either. So she understood where his life had been back then.

Lucas hadn't wanted to be the outcast, he'd said as much. So obviously this mind-reading thing was not a ploy for attention. He had to have really believed it himself.

But why had he suddenly lost his supposed abilities at the very time she turned up on the scene? Weirder and weirder.

Teal ducked in and out of the shower. By the time she'd dried off, her mind was back on the investigation.

That was when she realized she'd forgotten to take the mud sample from the victim's boots into the lab for analysis yesterday. Her brain must've been so consumed with her body aches that she'd hadn't thought of it at all.

Well, no problem. The lab was only fifteen minutes away. She'd zip down there in her Bureau-requisitioned sedan, drop off the sample and then come right back here for a nap. Twenty-four hours late to the lab was no big deal, anyway. The lab was probably backed up at least that far.

After a moment's indecision, she decided to put on a nicer pair of black slacks and a long-sleeved white shirt. Just in case someone from her office spotted her going into the lab. She tried never to be caught in public without wearing the good old Fibby uniform.

Digging around in the bottom of her closet, Teal found the khaki pants she'd had on the night of her mountainside slide. The pants probably needed to be pitched. The rump was split open and the knees were shredded. But in the front right pocket, Teal found the clear plastic evidence envelope with the mud sample.

Good to go. She tore out the front door with her car keys in one hand and the plastic bag in the other.

*Danger! Do not drive that automobile.*

Who'd said that? Teal stopped dead in her tracks and swung around, fully expecting to see the speaker standing nearby. But she was all alone in her front yard with the empty car.

Gulping back a lump that had formed in her throat and rubbing the chill-bumps off her arms, she took another step toward the driver's door of the sedan.

*Do not go. Danger.*

Where was that voice coming from? Teal prayed she wasn't hearing voices from her imagination. Had she hit her head on the way down the mountainside? Was she having a hallucination caused by the old grandmother's medicines?

She blinked her eyes and swiped her hand over them to make sure she was awake and not dreaming. The voice was indistinct, but nevertheless, the meaning was as clear as the autumn skies.

Looking around once more, she squinted to study the stand of tall cottonwood trees behind her rented mobile home. The trees swayed in the slight breeze and she could hear the leaves rattling like someone crumbling paper.

A few birds circled above the trees and a couple more were sitting on the apex of her roof. Other than that, not a living soul seemed to be around. Even the highway in front of her house was quiet for the middle of the morning.

This was ridiculous. She must be daydreaming. Tightening her grip on the keys, she moved to the car's door.

## *Chapter 8*

Lucas drove down the long, lonely stretch of two-lane blacktop that was known locally as Owl Springs School Road. He'd already passed the cutoff leading out through silver mesquite and creosote bushes over to the Raven Wash Medical Clinic that his cousin, Ben Wauneka, was temporarily running.

But Lucas was not going to the clinic today. He was on his way back to his grandmother's meadow. Back home. He'd driven this road a million times, and usually he loved to watch the pale tan-and-gray scenery of eroded gullies and dry arroyos go by his window. But today, even the blue-green vistas of the Lukachukai Mountains up ahead gave him no comfort.

It would take another forty-five minutes to reach his studio, and with every mile he became more and more convinced that going home would mean being too far away from Teal. But he didn't dare go back now. She would freak if she caught him checking up on her.

No. He would try to concentrate instead on what kind of a Dineh could've committed the murder.

A Navajo who didn't want to be discovered? Had a Dineh member killed out of fear? It was possible but not likely.

Even if such a Navajo had moved out of *hozho,* out of harmony with his spirit, he would not have committed the crime with a white man's weapon. A knife or a shotgun blast would've been more a Dineh's weapon of choice rather than the small-caliber pistol that had been used to kill the man.

Lucas glanced to his right and noticed a dozen raptors off in the distance, circling their supper on the desert floor. So many birds of prey at one time was not the way of nature, he knew. Just the same as the .22 gun had not been the Navajo way.

The sun dropped behind a cloud and Lucas slowed the SUV. Something was definitely wrong. He could feel it.

He pulled off to the side of the isolated road and stepped outside. Was there something wrong with his vehicle?

As he walked around, checking out the tires, Lucas began to wonder if someone he cared about was in trouble. This feeling of concern was quickly turning into overwhelming panic.

Could it be his grandmother who needed him? Hating that he could not simply "see" what the trouble was, Lucas pulled out his phone and called his grand-mother.

She was home but annoyed at being bothered when she'd been tending to her herb garden. Just as he was about to dial the Brotherhood number of Hunter Long to check on his other warrior cousins, two hawks split off from the circling raptors and headed straight for him.

"Brother Dineh," one of them said as he landed on the SUV's roof a few feet away. "I am known as *Accipiter striatus*. I am *of* the Sharp-Shinned Hawk Clan, born *for* the Bird People. I have taken over *Hastiin Hawk's* duties as warrior general of our allied armies."

"Hastiin Hawk is no longer chief?"

"He was lost in a battle with renegade vultures."

"Skinwalkers. I'm sorry to hear that. He was a good friend."

"We have come to warn you. The female who you defend is in danger."

"Um… The young woman? The FBI agent?"

"The woman you call *Bright Eyes*. You must protect her. She does not see and must not drive. Her road machine has been sabotaged."

"What? How do you know that?"

"*We saw.* We tried to warn the woman, but she does not listen as you do."

"You can talk to her? The same way you do to me?"

"*The same.*"

Lucas was surprised, but less panicked than he had been a minute ago. He put thoughts of why the Bird People could talk to Teal when they'd never before been able to talk to anyone but him into the back of his mind.

He would call Teal and tell her not to get into her car until he got back there and checked it out. She should be asleep now anyway.

"*Go now.* She does not listen."

"Now? You said you tried to talk to her. Hell, is she going to drive the car—now?"

"*Danger.*"

Lucas jumped into his SUV and pulled back out onto the blacktop, turning in as tight a U-turn as he could manage.

Damn the woman. She had promised to rest.

Presuming she had not been killed in a car accident or an explosion first, Lucas swore to wring her neck as soon as he got back there—right after he kissed her senseless.

He roared into Teal's front yard, mostly riding on the two left-side wheels. The trip that had taken him close to half an hour out took only about fifteen minutes back.

His satellite phone was burning up from his frantic efforts to reach Teal by phone. No answer. Was she gone? Asleep? Dead?

*Teal.* Her car was sitting right where it had been when he'd left forty-five minutes ago. It looked just the same. Obviously no explosions had happened and Teal could not have driven it away with any hidden defect if it was still here.

Had the Bird People been lying to him? That certainly seemed unlikely. They had no motive for betraying their Brotherhood allies.

Jumping out with his engine still idling, Lucas headed for her front door, calling her name over and over as he went. Where was she? Sound asleep?

If she was still okay, he had just learned a good lesson. No matter what she said in the future, he was not going to leave her alone again until the murderer had been caught.

"Teal," he shouted as he banged on her front door. "Bright Eyes, answer me."

"What's all the screaming about?"

It was Teal's voice. But the sound seemed to be coming from the direction of her car. No way. It was sitting turned off and vacant.

"Where are you?" he said as he jumped down from her front stoop and dashed over to the sedan to check it out.

At that moment a pair of feminine shoes poked out from under the car. Next came shapely legs clothed in sharp-creased black pants. Finally, the rest of Teal appeared as she climbed out from underneath her sedan.

The white blouse she had on was filthy, and a spot of purple fluid dotted the tip of her nose. He had never been so glad to see anyone in his whole life.

"What's the big deal?" she asked him as she tried to clean off her hands with a dirty rag.

"You're okay." He grabbed her up, torn between killing her on the spot and dragging her inside to make love.

"Hey," she complained. "I *am* okay. What's the matter with you?"

He plastered her face with kisses and held her tight, waiting for his heart to start up again.

"You're going to get yourself all dirty," she said as she pushed herself out of his arms. "What are you doing back here anyway? I thought I sent you home."

Lucas gulped in a breath. "And I thought you were going to rest. What are you doing all dressed up and hiding underneath your car?"

Looking up into his panicked face, Teal realized that the panic was directed at her. He must've felt something was wrong and raced back to find out for sure.

"I wasn't hiding. Someone tampered with my car. Probably last night while I was away. I'm no real crime scene expert, but this looks like a case of attempted murder to me."

"You discovered something wrong?"

"Oh, yeah. The automatic braking system sensor wire was disconnected. Then whoever wanted me dead reconnected the wire after adding a thin piece of plastic underneath the connector. We learned all about this trick in training. It disables both the system and the sensor lights so the brakes will fail with no warning."

"Was there brake fluid on the ground? A loose wire? How did you know what to look for?"

Teal almost opened her mouth to tell him that she'd heard warning voices in her head. But just in time she thought better of it.

She decided to turn the questioning back around to

him. "Why are you back here? Did you 'see' the trouble in your head?"

Not wanting to suggest that it might have been him who had disabled her car and then come back to make sure it had worked, she didn't want to push him too hard. He was one of the good guys, of that she was positive by now.

Taking her by the elbow, he began dragging her towards the front door. "If someone wants you dead, you make a terrific target standing out here in the open like this. I'll explain when we get you safely back inside."

"All right," she muttered. "I have to call the evidence team anyway. And now I guess I need another shower."

Fuming, Teal folded her arms over the fishbowl balanced in her lap and turned to stare out the SUV's passenger-side window. It had been a long, frustrating few hours since she'd discovered her car had been tampered with.

The FBI evidence team had showed up within minutes of her call—along with her boss. Shortly after that, Councilman Ayze, Director Sam and a raft of Navajo bigshots showed up in her front yard for an impromptu meeting of minds.

They'd eventually come to the conclusion that her life was in too much danger to allow her to continue with the investigation. They were just about to take it away from her and turn it over to Special Agent Kody

Long, when Lucas stepped in and convinced them she should be allowed to continue what she had started.

She'd be grateful to him some day, too. Whenever she quit being so furious she could skin him alive.

After another hour's worth of discussion with the bigshots, it was decided she would remain in charge of the investigation—but with stipulations. She could not stay at her own place for the duration of the investigation. Its location was obviously too well-known. And she was ordered to have at least one Dineh member with her at all times. Night and day.

Guess who volunteered himself and his guest bedroom for the job?

"You're not really still mad at me, are you?" Lucas slanted a glance in her direction as he drove them down the washboard gravel road on the way to his house.

She blew out a breath. "Why should I be mad? You saved my job."

"Well, yes. But..."

"I must admit," she interrupted. "I'd be a whole lot more comfortable if my fish wasn't packed up and if all my worldly possessions weren't stuffed into the back of this SUV. More comfortable if I could just go on home tonight to my own bed.

"Did you have to be so quick to volunteer?" she asked rhetorically. "Maybe if no one had stepped forward to take me in, they would've let me stay at home."

"Now, Bright Eyes, you know that wasn't going to happen. It's too dangerous there. If I hadn't offered, you would've lost your assignment—and your house would've still been too dangerous to stay in. You know that's the truth."

"Why is your place any safer than mine?"

He tsked, as if explanations should be unnecessary. "Your rental house is right on a major highway with nothing but a scrawny patch of cottonwoods to offer protection. My home is way off the beaten path on a rise overlooking my grandmother's meadow, and has natural protection from a cliff directly behind the house.

"Plus," he added. "My house has had curing ceremonies done to make it safer. And then, there's also my grandmother right down the road who can foresee trouble in the future."

"Right. Silly me. I should have known. My weapons and training are no match for a *farsighted* little old lady and a stony shrimp-colored cliff."

"Teal. What changed? Just a few hours ago you said you were glad we'd be riding together."

"Riding together. *Not* living together."

"You'll be comfortable at my place. I swear. It's for the best. You'll see."

He'd said it like that was the end of the discussion. And Teal supposed he was right. There was no way out of this mess now. She might as well shut up and make the best of it.

A few hours later, after Lucas had tucked her stuff into his tiny spare bedroom, he sat watching Teal as they both sipped after-dinner coffees at his dining-room table. She'd quit being mad at him right after he'd made

NO POSTAGE
NECESSARY
IF MAILED
IN THE
UNITED STATES

# BUSINESS REPLY MAIL

FIRST-CLASS MAIL    PERMIT NO. 717-003    BUFFALO, NY

POSTAGE WILL BE PAID BY ADDRESSEE

SILHOUETTE READER SERVICE

3010 WALDEN AVE

PO BOX 1867

BUFFALO NY 14240-9952

# Get FREE BOOKS and FREE GIFTS when you play the...

## LAS VEGAS

### GAME

*Just scratch off the gold box with a coin. Then check below to see the gifts you get!*

**YES!** I have scratched off the gold box. Please send me my **2 FREE BOOKS** and **2 FREE GIFTS** for which I qualify. I understand that I am under no obligation to purchase any books as explained on the back of this card.

## 340 SDL ELS3        240 SDL ELXF

| | |
|---|---|
| FIRST NAME | LAST NAME |

ADDRESS

| | |
|---|---|
| APT.# | CITY |

| | |
|---|---|
| STATE/PROV. | ZIP/POSTAL CODE |

(S-RS-03/07)

| 7 | 7 | 7 | Worth TWO FREE BOOKS plus TWO BONUS Mystery Gifts! |
|---|---|---|---|
| 🍒 | 🍒 | 🍒 | Worth TWO FREE BOOKS! |
| 🔔 | 🔔 | ♣ | TRY AGAIN! |

www.eHarlequin.com

Offer limited to one per household and not valid to current Silhouette® Romantic Suspense subscribers. All orders subject to approval.

her lamb chops and strawberry shortcake for dinner. She looked so beautiful sitting there that he barely noticed the tiny lines and purple smudges around her eyes.

But he did notice. And vowed that tonight she would be getting a full night's sleep. With *no* interruptions.

She never had gotten that nap today. And he'd never given her an answer about how he'd known she might be in trouble.

He'd thought all afternoon and evening about what to say. Should he try to explain about talking to the Bird People?

His gut said no. She would only come to the conclusion that he was even stranger than before.

But his heart said yes. He wanted her to know everything about him. More, he desperately wanted her to be the only one who truly understood him.

"So… You never answered me about how you knew to come back to my house this morning. If you're not getting your sight back, what made you turn around?" Teal tilted her head and the corners of her mouth cracked up in a half smile.

See there? They were already thinking alike.

She had taken the news about the Skinwalkers quite well. And the Bird People said she could've heard them talking if only she would've listened. That made her special—like him.

And perhaps worth the chance.

"This is going to sound crazy…"

She smothered a laugh. "No, really?"

"You're a laugh riot, Bright Eyes," he said with a forced smile. "You want to hear the truth or not?"

With a wide flourish, she turned her palm up and raised her eyebrows, urging him to continue.

"Fine," he muttered. "But so help me, if you even make one sound that resembles a snicker, you're dead meat."

She crossed her forefinger over her heart. "Promise."

Okay this was it, now or never. "Look, Teal, for the last several years I've lived up in these hills all alone except for my grandmother. I run through the woods near here alone in the early mornings for my daily training. About two years ago I noticed something odd while I was out there."

How would she take what came next?

Saying nothing, she let him hang himself with his own story. Everything he had ever said to her probably seemed odd.

"At first the birds, mostly the hawks and eagles, started following me as I ran," he began again. "Not like they were trying to get me out of their nesting territory or anything. But like they were just checking up on me. Watching out for me."

"Uh-huh."

"Just listen. After a few weeks, they started showing up everywhere I went. If I was outside working with the sand or at silversmithing, they would sometimes even land on my head.

"It spooked me for a while. I felt like I was living in some horror movie where the birds are out to get the humans." He stopped to watch her reactions. She was listening carefully and not laughing.

Here went all or nothing. "Then one day, one of the biggest hawks spoke to me. At first I thought it was all in my head. At that time, the noise from other peoples' thoughts was deafening sometimes. But this creature wasn't human, and it wasn't just in my mind."

Teal said nothing and gave no indication of what she was thinking. It was one of those rare moments when Lucas would've killed to get his old gifts back.

"Now it seems," he continued, not knowing what else to do. "The Bird People have turned out to be good allies for the Brotherhood—it's that Citizen's Watch committee I was telling you about, remember?"

"Hold on a minute."

Uh-oh. He could visualize bad jokes coming right up ahead.

"You explained that *Bird People* term before, but you didn't mention they were your allies," she said with a completely straight face. "What kinds of things do you do for each other?"

"Are you making fun? You promised."

"Not at all. I want to know."

"It'll take a bit of explaining. You want some more coffee?"

She nodded and he poured her another cup from the rapidly cooling carafe.

When they settled down again, he began. "I wouldn't mention this to a stranger. But you are no longer strange to me."

He saw her bite her lip to keep in the smile. Still,

she stayed quiet, took a sip of coffee and let him continue.

"There's a secret war going on across Dinetah, Teal. I am one of…"

"War?" she interrupted as she sat straight up in her chair. "What kind of war? Why doesn't the Bureau know about it?"

He waffled his hands, palms down in a placating gesture. "Calm down. I said it was *secret*. There's a good reason why we don't want outsiders to know. Give me a chance to explain."

She flopped back against her chair and let out a breath. "This had better be good. You've really gotten off topic here. But this new war stuff may make for a good story."

"You're being judgmental again, Bright Eyes. But I'll agree that it's hard to accept some things until you see them with your own eyes.

"I'll start at the same place where I came in," he continued. "Several years ago, a woman who was then known as the Plant Tender—the person who helps gather the herbs and potions for Dineh medicine men—went to a cousin of mine, Dr. Ben Wauneka, with a fantastic story. Ben's both a *hataalii*, a trained medicine man, and a licensed medical doctor. So he's pretty skeptical about things.

"Well, the Plant Tender told him that she'd discovered a terrible truth." Lucas hesitated to say these things to Teal. But he'd started so there was no choice except to finish.

He took a slug of cold coffee and began again. "It

seems a mystery man, who'd seemingly come out of nowhere, had taught himself a few of the ancient Navajo witchcraft secrets. And he'd formed a new cult of Skinwalkers in Dinetah.

"Worse than any of the previous Skinwalker cults that have shown up in our land throughout history, this one uses modern technology combined with those old secrets in order to cheat, steal and grab power from the People."

"And this bad guy is still out there?" she interjected again.

Studying her for a second, Lucas decided she was dead serious and not trying to be funny. "We've tried to catch him and have been close several times. But his power is strong and he sends lackeys to do all his dirty work. We've taken custody of Skinwalker warriors throughout the years. But every time, the ones we capture die mysterious deaths that we know are the Wolf's doing. We've never been able to interrogate any of them.

"All we really know," Lucas continued. "Is that this guy has mastered taking the form of the Navajo Wolf. The People have always considered the Wolf to be the worst of the evil ones."

Teal looked skeptical, but she let him continue.

"We also know that his underlings can change their shapes, too. They have appeared as snakes, ravens, mastiff dogs and vultures. All legendary witch figures for Navajo traditionalists.

"But back to my involvement with the Brotherhood. My cousin Ben became convinced that the Plant

Tender was right. The two of them decided to form a strategic alliance of good Dineh medicine men to fight off the evil ones. Ben began asking men he felt he could trust, his own clan cousins, to join a secret brotherhood in order to fight the scourge."

"Why not just go to the cops? The FBI?"

Just listen to her, Lucas thought. Teal was actually asking questions that sounded like she might be taking his story seriously. What a woman.

"Several reasons," he said. "First off, if I came to your boss with this story, what do you think he'd have to say about it?"

"Chris?" Teal gave that a moment's consideration. "Chris would think you were nuts. Probably have you locked up for psychiatric observation."

"Yeah," he agreed. "The Navajo Tribal DPS would no doubt be more receptive because they've grown up knowing about Skinwalkers. In fact, my cousin Hunter Long is a tribal cop and he's one of our Brotherhood warriors. But there's not much the police can do to help us with this war, so we keep the knowledge of it limited to a few people."

"Why can't they help you? What does it take to fight off these bad guys? A stake through the heart or maybe garlic necklaces?"

"Bad joke, Bright Eyes. Actually, the old Plant Tender dug up an ancient piece of knowledge about how to combat the terror. Now the Brotherhood has special medicine-man chants that can weaken the Skinwalkers enough for us to fight them off with guns and knives as if they were real humans."

"You said the *old* Plant Tender. What does that mean? How old?"

"The old Plant Tender died in battle with the Skinwalkers. We now have a *new* Plant Tender who helps us gather and take care of our sacred plants."

"She died? Really? How?"

"She was attacked by Skinwalkers who had turned into vultures and a raven."

"Oh, come on now. I've listened to your story patiently, but expecting me to accept that is ridiculous."

"I saw it, Teal. With my own eyes."

"Right," she said with a wry grin. "So what does any of this have to do with the Bird People? And more to the point, with how you knew to come back to check up on me?"

"The Bird People have become our allies in the war. They've helped us many times. They even assisted by killing off the vultures that attacked the Plant Tender."

"And…?"

"And I am their contact in the Brotherhood. They talk to me and I…"

"Oh, crap. They really talk to you? Hell, then it must be true."

# Chapter 9

"What do you mean? Did you hear the Bird People talk?"

Teal cringed inside. Damned man was going to make her explain the whole thing, wasn't he?

She shrugged as if it meant nothing. "I didn't think it was the birds at the time. Even now, I suspect I was dreaming. Birds do *not* talk to people in real life."

Lucas sat there across the table, staring at her with obvious empathy and companionship in his eyes. Two of a kind, he must be thinking. Two weirdos who can hear birds speaking English.

Well, she wasn't ready to be labeled a nutcase. Not yet anyway.

Turning the conversation, she tried to find out how serious Lucas was about hearing the birds. "So...

You're saying that the birds told you to turn around and come back? How'd they know the ABS brakes had been tampered with?"

"Their leader told me they *saw* someone sabotage your car."

"Oh? Who was it?"

"They didn't say."

"No, of course not. I don't suppose I'll be able to interrogate this leader of theirs, either, will I?"

"Maybe. We can ask him the next time we see him."

"You can't call them up? Uh, with a bird caller or whistle or something?"

"It doesn't seem to work that way. They've always just shown up when they were needed."

"Right."

"Look, Teal. I admit this is a tough concept. But we're not crazy. There's two of us now who can hear them. I can speak to them, too. Maybe we'll find out that you have that same gift.

"But it doesn't make us both nuts," he assured her.

"No? Then what does it make us?"

"Just a little different than the others." He reached across the table and covered her hand with his. "But we're in this together. We'll have each other to discuss things with."

Teal took a deep breath and tried a watery smile. For a brief second she wondered if Lucas's grandmother had been feeding them both hallucinogens. It didn't seem likely. But from now on, she was going to be a lot more careful about what she had to eat and drink.

* * *

The next morning, Teal stuffed the last of her Burger King breakfast sandwich into her mouth and washed it down with stale coffee. She was riding in Lucas's SUV as he drove them toward the Black Mesa mine to interview one of the managers. They still had a good hour to travel, even after they'd left the fast-food place in Chinle, Arizona.

After a decent night's sleep, she woke up having come to a conclusion. She was *not* crazy. And she had not heard birds talking, either, no matter what Lucas said.

What she'd heard in her head were her own cop's gut instincts telling her to be careful. Simplest answer, if you thought about it rationally.

Which was not easy while she was hanging around Lucas.

The animal magnetism he gave off seemed to be turning her brain to mush. She'd come to another conclusion, too. There *would* be more times for them to be together sexually before her investigation was over. After all, she was living under his roof.

She wanted one more time between them, so there would be. In the meantime, the two of them would not be talking about any of those woo-woo things he believed in so fervently. She was afraid to tell him what she really thought about them. That could be a huge turn-off to their budding sexual relationship.

She crammed the empty breakfast bag under her seat and propped her feet up on the dashboard. With every mile that passed by her window, the scenery seemed to make another drastic change.

It was all vast, to be sure. Lots of open space. Lots of nothing but rocks and brush. But it was *ever-changing* rocks and brush.

Every spread-apart farm or ranch or whatever they called them seemed very much like the last one, however. There would be one big house on the property with one or two of those eight-sided outbuildings alongside it. Old cars scattered around throughout the yards, some of them up on blocks. Every house had a basketball hoop stuck high on either a telephone or electric pole. And most even had a similar rusty yellow school bus parked somewhere nearby.

The farther they traveled, the more she noticed the sweeping beauty of the land. They were driving on a semidesert, high plateau, and it was easy to see water would be precious in this kind of environment.

"How much rain do they get around here?" she asked.

"Not a lot. Between seven to twelve inches a year. There's an underlying groundwater source that keeps springs alive for the People and their animals in between rains. It's called the Navajo Aquifer."

"No wonder we haven't seen very many houses along here. There wouldn't be enough water for everyone."

"There still isn't enough water. Some people have to have their drinking water delivered by truck.

"But that isn't the only reason the houses are far apart," he continued with a completely straight face. "There's an old joke that says we build our houses far apart because we Navajos don't like living near Navajos."

A laugh erupted from her mouth before she could call it back. She was going to have to get used to Lucas's wry and dry sense of humor.

The road took a wide curve and up ahead was a stop sign. They hadn't seen any sign of life at all for about fifteen minutes. But now they turned onto a major blacktopped highway, U.S. Route 160.

"We're a few minutes out of Kayenta," Lucas told her. "Would you mind if we stopped there for coffee?"

"Not at all. I'm getting hungry, too."

"Again?"

She threw him a disgruntled look. "Feed the lawmen when they're hungry or pay the consequences, buster."

His lips narrowed, but his eyes crinkled up in a smile. Maybe Lucas would have to get used to her wry and dry sense of humor, too.

As they traveled southwest, Teal noticed another big change in scenery. One side of the road, the north side, had become wild-looking desert with a deep, narrow arroyo carrying a small amount of water at its bottom, and behind that was a high ridgeline. The hills that made up the ridge and ones that could be seen behind those were monstrous bluffs and buttes of every pink-orange hue she'd ever seen.

"Look there at the small herd of whitetail deer, Bright Eyes."

"Wow. How do they live out here?"

"The arroyo carries enough water to maintain a kind of plant life, even in this desert."

Teal had also started noticing the other side of the road, where taller plants than she'd seen before were growing in profusion. That side's scenery wasn't nearly as wild as the other, but it was still empty of structures. All that could be seen were waist-high sage, cedar and juniper trees. Yellow flowering bushes at least six feet tall brightened up the otherwise gray-green vistas, but she couldn't name any plant that would flower so brilliantly in the fall.

The outskirts of a town came into view and she and Lucas began reading the billboards for places to eat in Kayenta.

"That nice motel up ahead has a good place to eat," Lucas told her. "We'll stop there."

"I'd rather we'd stop at the drive-in advertised down the road. I haven't seen one of those old fashioned eat-in-your-car places in years."

"Aren't you tired of sitting in the car?"

"Nope."

They stopped at the drive-in, and though each ordered quite differently, Teal and Lucas were fairly happy with their choices.

Once they'd finished eating, Teal squirmed around and began locking her seat belt down for the next part of the trip. "Ugh," she muttered when her bottom leaned on something with rough angles.

"What's the matter?"

She reached under her back end, but finally figured out that what she was sitting on was something in her own pocket. Pulling the plastic envelope free, she remembered that these were yet another pair of unwashed jeans. One of these days she was going to be forced into doing more laundry than just rinsing out her underwear.

"It's the evidence envelope with the mud scrapings from the dead man's boots," she told him. "I tried to give it to the crime scene supervisor at my house yesterday. But he told me his team had gathered plenty of evidence from the dead man's body already and still had his shoes to work on."

"They didn't need that sample, then?"

"No. But I forgot to throw it away."

"Don't." Lucas took the plastic envelope from her hands and stared at the mud inside. "This is unique mud. Have you had a chance to really study it?"

"I'm not sure I would've known what I was looking at even if I'd had time."

He smiled at her and held up the envelope. "See those sparkly particles sprinkled through the reddish mud that's rapidly drying?"

"Yeah. What is it?"

"I'm not sure. Looks like…" He hesitated. "I need a second opinion. Let me call the friend in the Navajo DPS I was mentioning earlier, Hunter Long. He's one of the best trackers in the West and knows this area better than anyone else. He's also in the Brotherhood. Mind if I have him meet us later?"

"Okay by me. If you think that's important."

"Remember, Bright Eyes. Water is scarce out here. If the one who died walked into mud right before he was murdered, then we need to find out where he was when it happened."

"Yes, I agree that would be worth a look if we can find it."

"Hunter Long will know where to look."

\* \* \*

Twenty minutes later, Lucas pulled the SUV off the side of the highway at the turnoff to Black Mesa. The foliage was denser here than it had been back up the highway at Kayenta, so he parked in the shade of a stand of Russian olive trees.

Hunter had promised to meet them within the hour and wanted to accompany them to see the mine manager. Lucas was glad for the extra company. It had been all he could do to keep his hands off Teal. With Hunter along, his mind could stay on things that were more important at the moment than his physical desires.

Ever since he'd touched her and tasted her for real instead of just in dreams, he could barely think of anything else. But he had to start thinking with his brain instead of with other parts of his body. The more he considered the method of the dead man's death and that someone had tampered with Teal's car, the more he was convinced all this was Skinwalker related.

But he couldn't prove it. They weren't using normal Skinwalker weapons or tactics.

"While we wait for your pal, you mind telling me what you know about the Black Mesa mine?" she asked out of the blue. "Explain the trouble to me so I know the right kind of questions to ask the manager."

Lucas would've rather she'd wanted to talk more about the Bird People. Or maybe more about the Skin-walkers and their war. But talking about anything was much preferable to sitting here wishing he could take her in his arms again.

"All right." His mind flashed on a picture of her face all flushed and rosy as he'd worked his tongue down her body. "Look off down the main highway. You see that green thing that sticks about fifty feet up in the air?"

"Huh?" She squinted off in the distance. "Hey, yeah. What is that? It looks like a giant caterpillar."

"It's the slurry conveyor for the mine. It actually runs for 273 miles. From the mine to the power plant. The last slurry line in the U.S." He watched her slender throat work as she swallowed and his hands began to shake.

"Ugly, isn't it?"

"You haven't seen an open-mine coal pit yet," he told her. "Now that's what I call ugly." The woman sitting beside him, however, was still a beautiful work of art in his opinion.

"Can you explain what a slurry line does?" She shifted in her seat and the white long-sleeved blouse she'd worn stretched across her breasts.

His heart thumped so loudly in his chest he was afraid she'd hear it and know how badly she was getting to him. That would not be good for their relationship.

"I can explain from the viewpoint of a Navajo," he managed after swallowing hard. "Good enough?"

"Sure. Go with what you've got. I'm supposed to be coming to you for that part anyway."

"Well, a coal-slurry line operates a lot like the old gold-mining lines did. After the coal rocks come out of the ground, they're ground up into nugget-size pieces as if they had been through a garbage disposal. Those nuggets are then mixed with water…lots of water. And the whole water/crushed-rock mixture is sluiced through that big over-ground pipeline you see up there."

"And it pushes it for 273 miles? That must take huge amounts of water."

"Yeah. That's where we come back to the Navajo point of view."

Teal's eyes widened and she heaved a sigh as she sat back to pay attention. He almost lost his entire train of thought. She had to stop looking and breathing like that if he was going to finish.

"Uh." He, too, shifted in his seat. "The coal mine and the electric plant it supplies employs hundreds of Navajo workers. And the People do need the work. Plus, the Navajo Nation as a whole earns millions a year in royalties from the coal-mine operation.

"But most environmentalists and traditionalists in the Nation would prefer it if the operators stopped tapping the underground aquifer for their slurry line. Our scientists have proven that's what causes water levels to drop."

"So…I imagine feelings run high on the subject," Teal said thoughtfully. "Economics versus health. Money talks, but without water there is no life."

"Right." He was amazed at how perceptive of his views she was for someone not raised on the reservation.

Was that their predestined connection at last showing up? The two of them fell into private thoughts, and Lucas once again wished he could read hers.

Why had he been dreaming about this woman for most of his life? It had to be more than just his destiny to protect her. That was already a given.

His emotions where she was concerned seemed confused and unclear. He wanted her, no question. He would protect her, no question about that, either. But what else was going on between them?

Just at that moment, a Navajo Nation police patrol unit pulled up behind them, and Hunter Long stepped out of the all-white SUV heading in their direction. Lucas put his confusion aside for the time being. What Teal needed from him now was his knowledge and protection.

*That* he could handle.


"Yes, I agree," Hunter said from the backseat of Lucas's SUV. "Those sparkly bits do look like gold flecks. Or maybe fool's gold."

"That's what I thought, too," Lucas agreed.

They were all still sitting in Lucas's SUV under the Russian olive trees with the windows rolled down. Teal had been fascinated by the Navajo tribal cop when she'd met him. A tall lean man, his long straight hair was pulled back in a bun at the nape of his neck and his skin was the same copper color as her own. But his eyes were a soft gray and they made him look like the half-breed she was sure he must be.

The overall picture Hunter projected was pure gorgeous. But still, he didn't capture her attention the way Lucas had right from the very moment she'd first seen him.

She must be slipping not to fully fantasize over such a fabulous hunk as Hunter, even considering that the man was wearing a gold band on the third finger of his left hand.

Finally, the words he'd said sank in to her daydreams. "Gold? Somewhere on the reservation? I thought you folks only mined oil, coal and uranium?"

"There's no substantiated gold," Lucas told her. "Nearly a hundred years ago now there were rumors of a lost gold mine. But it was never found. Most people think the thing was simply a big hoax."

"Most people do," Hunter agreed. "But not all of us."

"Really? Do you know where it is, then?" Teal wasn't interested in gold, but a lost mine might be a good spot to check for suspicious activity.

Hunter shook his head. "As much as I've been out on the land, I've never spotted anything that would even resemble a gold mine. But I do have a few ideas about where one might look."

"We're running short of time right now, Cousin," Lucas said. "But when Teal is finished with her interview at the Black Mesa mine, maybe you can go over a Dinetah map with us. We'd like you to point out all the places near Black Mesa where water can be found at the surface during this time of year."

"Yes, I can do that. And I'll mark off a few places that might also have hidden gold along with the wet spring or seep. You can hunt there first."

A short time later the three of them were standing amidst huge rolls of orange-colored cable at the central warehouse for the Black Mesa mining company and talking to Micah Taylor, one of the mine's managers.

A blond man with a large hooked nose and ruddy complexion, Taylor seemed to be answering the questions as truthfully as he could. "We've had legitimate environmental protestors around the mining operation for as long as I can remember. But these new so-called accidents have only been happening for the last few months."

"I've read some of the reports," Teal told him. "But can you tell us all again what kind of accidents you're talking about?"

"Oh, they don't really look much like accidents. Whoever is responsible wants to be sure we know it's being done on purpose. It's crazy stuff, like a supposed freak lightning strike on a records shack that burned the place to the ground. And like a rusted-out spot on a metal shaft that had just been inspected. Then last week, one of our cables snapped and sent three men to the hospital. We'd never had a bad cable break before in the entire history of this mine."

"Had you ever met the man who was murdered? Eddie Cohoe was his name."

Taylor smirked at her. "Yeah, I heard you were now

the fed in charge of the murder investigation. I guess the whole reservation has heard about you by now."

"Can you please just answer the question?"

"Sure. I knew Eddie. He stopped in to see me a few weeks ago. Wanted to tell me he was investigating the accidents for the Navajo Tribal Council. I guess he imagined himself to be undercover or something, but apparently he wasn't under far enough."

Hunter took a step closer to the mine manager. "If the Tribal Council had thought it was going to be that dangerous for a man to infiltrate an environmental group, they would've sent a lawman with more experience. Before your men ended up in the hospital, a few inconvenient accidents would not normally have suggested murder was next on the agenda."

"I didn't mean to sound like a smart-ass, Officer Long. I wasn't suggesting he brought on his own demise or anything. It's just…"

Lucas also stepped closer to the tight little group and tried to encourage the Anglo manager to continue with his thought. "Just what?"

"Well, I told Eddie this same thing. A few of the accidents were, I dunno, *strange*."

"Strange how?"

"Somebody managed to tamper with our property while it was being closely guarded. Or, they did it while security alarms were in place and operating just fine. One of the cases happened when a guard with a dog was on duty and he never heard or saw a thing. Weird stuff like that.

"It bothered me at the time. One of my guys was

joking about ghosts being responsible—or maybe that a superhuman flew in, did the damage and flew back out again. Real creepy stuff."

Teal noticed Hunter and Lucas surreptitiously throwing each other cautionary glances. She knew exactly what they were thinking. But she had no intention of letting talk of witches interrupt her investigation.

Instead, she asked the manager if he knew the leaders of the environmentalist groups that frequented picket lines or community meetings concerning the mine. The manager gave her a couple of names and then excused himself to go back to work.

On their way back to Hunter's car, Teal decided she needed to mention witchcraft to these two Navajos and get her feelings on the subject out in the open.

"You two are thinking it had to be those Skin-walker dudes that perpetrated those strange accidents, aren't you?"

Lucas opened his mouth to make a comment, but Hunter spoke up first. "Be careful throwing words around that may be dangerous for you, Special Agent Benaly. Our cousin tells me he has explained the war to you so you will not make rash statements when talking to the People. I would heed his advice if I were you."

Teal almost made a smart remark back to the tribal cop, but changed her mind. She didn't need to make an enemy out of any of Lucas's friends. Not in the middle of a tricky investigation anyway.

She opened her mouth and stuck her foot in it

instead. "Can either one of you please tell me why just being able to change over to animal form should be so bad? All you people love animals, don't you?"

Lucas hesitated. "The way we understand it is hard to put into words. But I guess I can say that changing over is bad simply because it's witchcraft. And witchcraft is a reversal of the Navajo Way. A witch is automatically out of *hozho,* out of balance, and needs to be made beautiful again."

"Besides that," Hunter interrupted to put in his own opinion. "These Skinwalkers are bad guys who change over only to do misdeeds. Like stealing and murdering. That should say it all."

That *should* say it all, Teal thought. But in her opinion, there was a lot more to be said on the subject.

Later. Much later, however, when she and Lucas could be alone and when he trusted her more than he did now.

Of course, there were a few other things that she wanted to say…or do…with Lucas first. But those would have to come later, too.

Much later. When *she* trusted *him* more.

## *Chapter 10*

Ten days later, after trekking to four rock-filled caves and interviewing five different environmentalists—a couple of whom were sharp activists and the rest wacko nutcases—Teal still wasn't clear on whether Lucas trusted her or not. And she was *definitely* waiting for a night of pleasure until she felt absolutely sure of him.

Today they were skipping interviews to go to two of the most distant potential water sources. Both of which Hunter felt also had the capability of being gold-mining spots.

"You sure these shoes will be okay on the rocks today?" she asked Lucas as the two of them headed down Navajo Route 98 toward Page, Arizona.

They weren't going all the way to Page and the

Navajo power plant, though. Today they were going off-road to scout a canyon that Hunter had marked on the map where the murdered man might have been walking in both mud and gold dust.

"Positive," Lucas said as he slowed the SUV. "I haven't been anywhere near Sour Water Canyon in years. But from what I remember, it's got more sand than it does granite or basalt, and more rounded hills rather than the steep slot canyons. Your shoes should be fine."

He watched her nod sharply at his remarks and knew she was remembering how he'd saved her life in Many Caves Canyon. Lucas was remembering it, too. And vowing to do everything in his power to keep her from harm today, as well.

She had been brightening his dull and lonely life. It was only fair that he could save hers. Actually, it seemed odd how her presence in his house and studio had suddenly made the place feel much more like a home. No one else had ever spent much time there.

Lucas always thought the reason for that was that everyone wanted to give him the time and space to be creative—to work on his art pieces. But now, he wondered if maybe the others just hadn't wanted to spend that much time there because of his differences.

Teal didn't seem to mind though. She'd made herself at home and seemed to love sitting outside under the cottonwoods and piñons, watching him at the silver forge. Her companionship had been hard to adjust to at first. But now he wondered how he would ever be able to go back to creating all alone.

She bent down to pull her BlackBerry out of her pack, then studied her electronic files for a moment.

Staring through the windshield at a distant eagle and several other raptors circling on a hunt out over the desert and canyons, Lucas began feeling completely comfortable for the first time in days. Oh, he still was a little unsettled and as turned on by being close to Teal as ever. But it was a nice day to be headed outside in the sunshine with such a beautiful and intelligent companion.

"How do you feel your investigation is going so far?" he asked her to keep his mind on the point.

"Not so hot, really. Not one of the people we've interviewed has had any idea who might be behind the 'accidents'—let alone who might have committed a murder."

"Yeah, well, I told you murder is not something any Dineh would ordinarily think to do.

"But what about Old Woman Tanchee Begay?" he steered the conversation back to Teal with the question.

"What about her? What's her real name anyway? I can't put 'Old Woman Begay' in my report."

"Sure you can. It's what she's known by. I told you about our childhood nicknames, didn't I? Well, sometimes we get a nickname later in life that sticks with us. I doubt if she even knows her Anglo given name anymore."

"Hmm. Sounds disrespectful."

"Believe me, calling someone old is a form of respect in a land as hard as ours."

"Whatever. The names wouldn't matter if we'd been able to get any useful information."

"What they told you was useful," he insisted. "Not one of those people has any idea who might've been causing the accidents. They all swear it isn't anyone in their respective environmental groups. And I believe them. Old Grandmother Tanchee Begay never lied a day in her life."

"You believe them, do you?" Teal said with a friendly roll of her eyes. "Are you reading minds again?"

"Not since you showed up," he admitted. "But I know you put a lot of faith in those gut instincts of yours. Let's just say that my instincts are working every bit as well as yours. None of those people was lying to you. They were all as surprised by the accidents as they were by the murder.

"That should be excellent information to have," he added wryly. "Isn't being able to eliminate suspects every bit as good as adding them to the list?"

She turned off her BlackBerry and jammed it into her backpack without a remark. Driving off the two-lane highway onto a private gravel road that would lead them to the canyon, Lucas tried to judge her mood.

He knew his mood had been becoming more and more irritable every day. Was she feeling the stress of their living and working close to each other without touching the same way as he was?

Lucas decided that later tonight he would speak to her about their growing relationship and where it was headed. He knew for sure where he wanted it to go. But…what did she want?

"Well, I'll be damned," Teal said as she jammed her hands on her hips and stared into the empty opening. "You think this is really it? We actually found the old lost gold mine?"

"Take it easy, Bright Eyes." Lucas had been hit by a sudden chilling premonition of darkness, even though the late-afternoon sun was still high and warm in the sky. "If the murder victim was killed here, maybe we should go slow."

"The place looks deserted. What could happen?"

"I just think it would be wise to be cautious, that's all. Some of the old gold-mine stories talked about booby traps—set by the prospectors to keep people from stealing their gold."

Bending to gather some wet sand and dirt, he crushed it in his palm. "Looks like we found the right spot. Hunter's map guess was right on. This mud is the same as what we found on the victim's boots. Same gold flecks and everything."

"Where's that water coming from anyway?" Teal asked.

A trickle of water was leaking right out of the side of the rocks at the mine opening. "It's known as a seep. Water naturally comes up from the Navajo Aquifer in spots. Sometimes it forms a spring, other times it just trickles out and forms mud."

Teal pulled her gun out of its holster at her back and used it to point toward the direction of the mine. "Booby traps or no, we need to check out the inside. I have a feeling about this place."

"You stay here and keep watch," he said as he

moved past her. "I'll check out the inside first and make sure it's safe."

"Hold it," she demanded. "I don't need you to make sure anything is safe. I can take care of myself. As a matter of fact, I took classes on the components of booby traps at Quantico.

"I do agree that one of us needs to stay out here and guard our backs, though." She used her free hand to flip out her flashlight. "So you stay here. I'll only be about ten or twenty minutes. Yell or whistle or something if anyone shows up."

Lucas was not at all happy about letting her go first. But she was a trained special agent. And it was vitally important that there be no possibility anyone could ambush them from behind.

So he stood at the mine entrance, with one foot in the shadow of the opening and one foot out in the sunshine. He would listen and watch in both directions.

Close by but hidden in the shadows, the Skinwalker Burrowing Owl set the last trick of his surprise. He was happy to have thought about doing this particular dirty deed when he had.

So what if one of these two Navajos was killed? They didn't matter in the larger scheme of things. All that mattered now was that the Navajo Wolf would be pleased by the chaos created if either an FBI agent or a Brotherhood warrior died today.

Searching the more intellectual side of his brain, the Burrowing Owl thought of one scenario that would be even more effective. What if both these two humans were somehow either physically or emotionally destroyed at the same time?

Wouldn't that be better yet?

Yes, he was sure it would be. He decided definitely to stick around and look for a good opportunity to cause even more damage. Flapping his wings silently in triumph, the Burrowing Owl slipped into his burrow and waited.

The minute Teal stepped into the darkness inside the mine opening, she knew they had found the right place. There was plenty of evidence that people had been here recently. In fact, judging by the litter scattered around the place, some group had been using this spot for meetings.

She flipped her flashlight beam out toward the distant reaches of the mine. It looked like this might've been a natural cavern originally; fingers of side caverns reached off into the dark oblivion.

Then, maybe a hundred years or so ago, someone had apparently converted it to a mining operation. More recently, like a few weeks or months ago, a table and chairs had been added about twenty-five feet inside the mine entrance.

Funny, none of the environmental groups she had interviewed would admit to knowing such a place as this existed. Obviously, judging by the wadded-up plastic wrappers, discarded plastic drink cups and twenty-four-ounce soda bottles, some group had met here not long ago.

A tiny scurrying noise sounded off in the far reaches

of the mine. A chill ran down her arms. *Bats?* Or mice maybe? Either way, Teal didn't much care for the idea.

"Teal, are you okay?" Lucas's voice echoed throughout the chamber from his spot at the entrance.

"Fine," she shouted back to him as she holstered her weapon. "Stay where you are. No one's hiding. But they've been here. That's for sure. I'm going back a ways to gather evidence."

"Don't go too far. It might not be safe. Why don't you let an evidence team do the gathering?"

She ignored him as she continued checking the rough floor and roof of the mine for booby traps. Moving slowly, she swung the flashlight beam around in a one-hundred-eighty-degree arch trying to spot any signs of tampering.

*Watch out. Go back.*

Teal spun around at the sound of the strange voice. That hadn't been Lucas's voice. It was too high-pitched and sounded very close by.

"Who's in here? Show yourself."

The minute she'd spoken the words, Teal knew the truth. The warning had been all in her head. There was no one else in the mine with her. She must be really spooked to start hearing voices in her head again.

From the mine opening, now nearly out of sight, came Lucas's voice calling out, "What did you say? Do you need me?"

"Stay there," she shouted. "I'm okay."

Taking a deep breath and straightening her spine, she took a few more steps and peered into the darkness ahead. Something shiny flashed in her beam, and about fifteen feet ahead was another pile of trash on the floor.

* * *

Lucas shifted his thoughts from worrying about what Teal might be facing to the autumn sun that was easing lower in the sky. During this season the grasses on the sheep plains were never the same deep green color as in the spring. They were a soft golden hue instead, and the sunsets were tinted a lavender-blue color with deep rose tendrils reaching out across the skies from west to east—more beautiful to his artistic soul than at any other time of the year.

Fall rains would be coming soon, at least to the western flank of the Chuska Mountains. The air and cloud formations were already starting to change.

Drawing on the Navajo Way, Lucas tried to make sense of the accidents that had been happening near the coal mines. He'd been taught that there is an order to everything, and he could find the reasons if he just looked for a pattern.

But there didn't seem to be any rhyme or reason for senseless accidents. Would environmentalists use vandalism tactics after years of openly and legally picketing the mines? That made no sense at all. Why now?

In fact, Lucas had heard rumors that the power plant would be shutting down soon. If that happened, there would probably not be any reason to keep the coal mines open at all. Simple economics would win the day for the people who really cared about the groundwater and the air surrounding the plant.

The more he thought about it, the more Lucas became

convinced that there was more to the accidents than simple protests. Where was the pattern? It seemed there was none. No pattern, no reason. Acts done for simple chaos.

*Skinwalkers!*

Turning toward the gold-mine entrance, Lucas began shouting, "Teal, get out of there. Now!"

He heard nothing.

Taking two hesitant steps inside the shadowed opening, he tried again. "Bright Eyes! Answer me or I'm coming in after…"

A bright flash of light and noise from an explosion interrupted his too-late warning. Hot orange-colored air, all smoky and dirty, blasted him in the face.

He coughed, sputtering blindly inside a filthy haze. Automatically stepping back, he covered his mouth and nose with his arm.

"Teal, are you okay?" he choked out after a moment. "Teal!"

By now the dust was beginning to settle and Lucas ran straight into the mine, shouting her name as he went. About twenty feet inside the opening he came to a halt at the results of the explosion. A cave-in. But how thick was the rubble? Could he dig his way through to her with just his hands?

Beginning to dig, he grappled with the dirt and rocks until his fingers were bloody and he could barely breathe anymore. Dashing back outside, he took a deep breath of fresh air and pulled out his satellite phone.

Lucas needed help. He needed the Brotherhood.

Teal dragged herself from the ground and dusted off. Slightly disoriented because of the darkness and the ringing in her ears, she went down on her knees and felt around looking for either her flashlight or the lantern she'd lit a few minutes ago. But everything was covered in a heavy layer of silt and dirt.

What had happened? Had that blast been a cave-in or maybe a booby trap that she'd missed?

Whatever it was, it seemed to have caused the ceiling of the mine to fall down somewhere between her and the mine entrance. She shook her head, trying to comprehend what that meant.

Teal understood immediately that she was cut off from Lucas and the sunlight. But by the time she found her flashlight and dusted it off, too, she knew there were far worse things than light to worry about.

She flipped her flashlight beam around and saw the wall of rubble between her and the mine opening. It looked as if the rocks and wooden beams from the ceiling were totally blocking her way out.

Good thing Lucas was outside when it happened. He *had* been outside the mine like he promised, right?

Of course he had. He was fine and probably out there this minute digging through the rubble to get her out.

*Claustrophobia?* No, no, no. She'd never been nervous about being cooped up before. She absolutely refused to start being upset by other things that may or may not be in her head at this stage. The voices she'd been hearing in her mind were bad enough.

Okay. So she was alive and well and not the least bit claustrophobic. Should she help herself get free by digging from this side?

Reaching as high as she could by standing on tiptoes, Teal began pulling dirt and rocks off the pile. But huge clouds of dust and dirt rained down on her.

That wasn't going to work. But right then, another far darker thought occurred to her.

*Air.* Was there going to be enough oxygen in this mine for her to wait for Lucas to break through the wall of rubble?

Oh. My. God. She was going to die. Suffocate to death.

*Move back into the cavern, Bright Eyes. There is air enough.*

Huh? Where was that voice coming from? It wasn't Lucas's voice, and that definitely was *not* all in her imagination.

"Who's speaking?" she asked to the darkness.

*"You will find more air. Step back."*

Well, as hot as she was, that voice had been chilling.

She threw the flashlight beam toward the back of the mine shaft. That voice couldn't be in her head. It just couldn't be.

Needing to think before she moved another inch, Teal halted but kept the light flitting around the cavern's shaft. The voice had called her Bright Eyes. Lucas was the only one who ever did that. Could it really be him? Was the man playing some horrible practical joke?

Or perhaps it was possible that he was sending her

messages by psychic power. Could he do that? Could he think of something and have it fly through space and land in someone else's head?

Oh, come on, Teal, she chided herself. That's not even close to possible.

But then, who was speaking?

She pulled her weapon from its holster again and pointed it out toward the darkness in the back of the mine. "I demand that you answer me. Who's here?"

*"Look up. You will see light and air."*

"You can't see air, for heaven's sake..." She still didn't know who was speaking. But she flashed her beam upward and did see a spot way up in the ceiling where a low, filtered light was coming through a tiny hole.

A way out? No. She immediately realized the hole was at least fifteen feet up and the sides of the mine shaft were not made for climbing. They were rough, but not rough enough to allow for footholds.

"Is someone up there? Can you get me out?"

Not a sound could be heard, save for the echoes of her own voice through the darkness. No help from that quarter. But at least she was not going to suffocate while she waited to be rescued.

She sat down directly under the airhole and turned off her flashlight to save the batteries. If someone else was in the mine shaft with her, she would hear them rustling around in the dark and her weapon was at the ready.

In the meantime, Teal wanted to consider what had happened. She was almost positive the explosion that caused the cave-in was not the result of natural earth shifting. It had sounded much more like a man-made bomb to her.

She searched her memory for any sound or unusual movements that she might have noticed right before the explosion. What or who had caused it?

Thinking back to what she'd been noticing right before the flash, she remembered the trash pile. Of course. She remembered her basic chemistry lessons on terrorist-style weapons from Quantico.

All you needed to make a bomb was aluminum foil, an empty two-liter soda bottle and bathroom drain cleaner. There had certainly been plenty of half-filled soda bottles lying around the ground at the time of the explosion.

But such bombs only had about a ten-minute timing delay after being set. She was sure she'd been alone in the mine for at least twenty minutes before the explosion.

Was someone else hiding inside this mine with her and she'd somehow missed him? Or had some bad guy used a radio or cell wave to set off the bomb? Such things were fairly easy for anyone who knew a little electrical engineering.

Wondering now whether her cell phone would work from this far underground, she pulled it out of her jacket pocket and flipped it open. No bars appeared. No service here.

And what was worse, her batteries were going dead.

And she was starting to become very thirsty.

And ravishingly hungry.

# Chapter 11

Lucas spun on the balls of his feet and stormed back into the mine. He had reached the Brotherhood by satellite phone only to find out that there was no one within an hour of his position. Kody and Hunter were both on the way, along with a rescue team from the Navajo Tribal Fire Department, but would Teal have enough air?

This was one of those times he'd mentioned to Teal when backup was too distant to be of much help. Nearly desperate with worry about her well-being, Lucas vowed that whatever it took, he would find a way of reaching her.

Digging into the dirt once again, Lucas ignored his bleeding hands and the lack of adequate fresh air in the tunnel. Absolutely positive that she was still alive and just on the other side of the debris, he refused to consider any other possibilities as he kicked at the heavy wooden beams that had fallen from the ceiling and created the rubble wall of her prison.

*Teal would make it out of this mine shaft alive.*

As he fruitlessly dug in the rock and dirt, Lucas tried to concentrate around his panic. Was there a chant he could use that might help her? What good was being a medicine man and having special gifts if you couldn't help someone you loved?

*Love.* Had he really just thought that word? It wasn't a concept he easily understood. For his whole life he'd wished only to be accepted. To become a friend instead of an outsider.

He was positive by now that he and Teal had become friends. But friendship was a far cry from something as lasting and overpowering as love.

Pushing the confusing thoughts from his conscious mind, Lucas stepped back to study the thick pile of debris. If he continued digging at the bottom, the entire wall of rock and wood could come down on him—or on Teal if she lay injured on the other side.

There must be a way to go about this in a smarter manner. He turned and ran out of the mine shaft. Determined to find a safer method of digging her free, he made the decision to run back to the spot where they'd left the SUV. It was parked a mile back down the hill on the last of the level ground. But a small shovel, blankets and extra water were stashed in the spare tire compartment. If he turned on the speed he could get there and back in under twenty minutes.

He hated leaving. Hated going any distance away without knowing for sure that Teal was alive. But this seemed the only real way of saving her life.

The decision made, Lucas Tso, champion Iron Man runner, took off down the sandy gravel hillside. If he managed his best mile-time, he wouldn't be gone for long. And this idea seemed to be her only hope.

Teal swiped the sweat out of her eyes and tried to concentrate on the airhole at the top of this shaft. Staring at it hard, she could swear she saw blue sky and passing clouds through that hole.

*Danger. You must go now.*

Oh, hell. The voices were back. She must be freaking out.

A smart comeback tumbled from her mouth. "If I could *go,* I sure as hell wouldn't be…" A cough and then a sputter were the next things out of her mouth.

Trying to take a deep breath of air to clear her throat, Teal quickly discovered why she'd been choking.

*Smoke!* There was a fire nearby. She sniffed now, trying to find out where the smell of smoke was coming from. And hoping like hell it wasn't coming from her lifesaving hole in the top of the shaft.

No, she realized as she heard a close crackling sound. The smoke was not coming from anywhere nearby. *It was here.* In the mine shaft with her.

She flipped the flashlight on and threw the beam toward the wall of debris behind her. Then she spotted it. Tiny orange embers in the middle of another pile of trash suddenly burst into tall flames right before her eyes.

How could it turn to full fire mode so fast? The embers couldn't have been smoldering for very long. She'd only just now noticed the smoke.

Racing over to the fire, she tried throwing sand and rocks on the blaze. But the more she worked, the worse the flames rose. The fire was totally out of control within seconds.

Now she allowed herself to panic.

"Help! Someone help me," she screamed uselessly. "Get me out of here."

*"Move back. Hurry."*

"Back where?" she shouted at the darkness.

*"Go now. The other way out."*

There was another way out? "How? Help me," she sputtered past another cough.

Hearing the flutter of wings, she cringed at the thought of bats in the shaft with her.

*"Move. Stay to the right."*

The heat from the flames was hot enough now to fry the clothes right off her body. Her eyes watered from the smoke. There wasn't much time to save herself.

So, bats or not. Spooky voices in the dark or not. Teal had little choice but to exercise some of her special agent's self-discipline, find the right side of the shaft wall and move away from the fire as fast as she could go.

Stumbling through the thick smoke, she managed to keep her feet under her as she scurried back down the dark mine shaft. Within ten yards, the wall she'd been following disappeared from under her fingertips. She found herself grappling about reaching for thin air.

"Now what? Tell me where to go," she choked as she took a few steps straight ahead.

*"Stay right."*

At this point she didn't give a rip who was speaking, just as long as they were telling her the truth. She fumbled back to the mine wall through the thick haze of foul smoke and discovered the shaft had taken a turnoff to the right. She followed it quickly.

Once she'd made the turn, Teal found the air becoming fresher. "I'm going to live," she mumbled aloud.

*"Keep moving, Bright Eyes. You will live. We have saved you."*

*We?* There was more than one other person in this mine shaft with her?

Teal shrugged off the concern not only for her safety from intruders, but also for her sanity. And using the flashlight beam pointed straight ahead, she picked up speed.

There was no time to consider the circumstances. Now was the time simply to save her own life.

Lucas was barely breathing hard as he topped a rise, approaching the gold-mine entrance located straight up the hill. He had the fold-up shovel in one hand and an ax in the other, and he'd even managed to throw a rope and tarp around his neck in case he needed them to get her out. He'd been gone for just under twelve minutes. Another hundred yards and he'd be there.

Glancing up to the sky, he noticed the last specks of an orange glow streaking out from the western sunset. The first of the evening stars could already be seen blinking in the northern sky.

What would he do when it became too dark in the tunnel to dig? He hadn't even considered bringing back a flashlight. But he did have matches. Maybe he could build a fire and find the right materials to make a torch.

At the thought of a fire, Lucas dragged in a deep breath and smelled smoke. Was his mind playing tricks?

He slowed his pace and looked around. Then he spotted it. A thin plume of smoke coming from the top of the hill above the mine shaft's entrance.

Wildfires were entirely possible this time of year, but there was little fuel in the way of brush or trees nearby. What caused the fire and how close was it?

A low buzz and a high nasal trumpeting coo-coo call sounded directly off to his left. He hesitated to look away from the mine and Teal's prison for even a moment, but finally he turned to the noise.

*"The smoke is from the mine shaft, Brother."* The raspy voice was coming from near the ground.

Lucas searched the shadows and spotted a burrowing owl emerging from his burrow in the rock. He was taken aback because he'd never before known an owl of any sort to talk to him. And the People had always considered the burrowing owl to be evil.

But as he stared down at the small, cute creature,

Lucas decided this particular bird must have come
with a message. Such an innocent-looking being
couldn't possibly have evil intentions.

"Have you been sent from the Bird People's army?"
he asked the owl.

*"I have come to offer assistance. The woman's
trouble could be fatal and she must be saved now."*

"But how?" Lucas demanded with a catch in his
voice. "What can I do to reach her?"

*"There is a way, Brother. But we must hurry. Even
now the smoke chokes her."*

"How? I'll try anything. Do anything. Help me."

*"A hole exists in the mine shaft. A hole not big
enough for a human."*

"But if it's not big enough, then she can't get out
that way and I can't get in."

*"Another solution will save the FBI woman."*

"What? Tell me." Lucas was screaming now.
Frantic and close to hysteria, he wanted to shake this
tiny creature who had supposedly come to help him.

*"You must use the power given only to you. The
power that your brother humans shun. You can change
over, enter through the hole and see well enough in the
dark to lead her to fresh air."*

That statement took Lucas a moment to process.
"What power?" He was ready to try any solution but
he had absolutely no idea of what the owl meant.

*"You alone can talk to the Bird People, Brother. You
alone can take the form of your allies."*

"What? No." Lucas's gut reaction was to try

anything else and not consider what this creature was suggesting.

Turning into another species was witchcraft and even such thoughts were considered taboo. He didn't dare.

"Is that possible?" he asked the owl with fear in his heart. "A human can become a bird. Just like that?"

*"No time left to question. The woman suffers."*

Torn and verging on panic over Teal's well-being, Lucas made a snap decision. The ramifications and regrets could come later.

"Help me," he begged the owl. "Whatever it takes. Help me to reach her."

*"Very well, human."* The owl ducked into the burrow, pulled out a leather pouch with its beak and dropped the thing at Lucas's feet. *"Take these herbs as I say the chant that will make it happen."*

Lucas never hesitated. He opened his mouth to down the herb potion he'd found in the pouch, while the owl spoke ancient words that Lucas had never heard before.

As a Dineh medicine man, he thought he'd heard every chant, every ceremony. But this one was something new. If he could've cleared his head of the fear for Teal, he might've tried memorizing the words. But as it was, he could scarcely breathe, let alone take the time to think.

As he swallowed the herb potion, his vision blurred. Gray, hazy edges took over his multicolored world.

Still the owl's chants went on and on. Lucas's every

muscle began to contract. He felt his body tighten, his arms and legs shrink.

Closing his eyes, he concentrated on what was happening to his body and felt every cell altering—changing to something—something not human. Then all of a sudden he felt intense pain, strong enough to double him over.

Lucas collapsed to the ground and moaned. Was he about to die? Had the owl poisoned him?

*"Get up, Brother Owl."*

Confused and disoriented, Lucas forced his eyes open. His world was no longer the familiar colorful place it had been just moments before.

*"Spread your wings,"* the burrowing owl demanded. *"Prepare to fly with me above the trees."*

Lucas did as he was told. With one flap, the complete feeling of exhilaration zinged throughout his body.

As a child he'd had an overactive imagination. Many times he'd tried to fly like his friends the birds. He had a few scars to prove it, too.

But by the age of ten, he'd channeled his imagination into creative work, his art, and forgotten all about a childhood spent daydreaming of soaring above the trees.

Now this owl was offering him a golden opportunity. Though the colors of the world he had always loved had disappeared, leaving him with black-and-white images that held no real appeal, he couldn't wait to fly.

After a few tentative tries, Lucas followed the owl into the air. Swooping and soaring on every updraft, he found himself enjoying the freedom of flight and becoming greedy for more and more air time.

On one daring glide, flying low against the treetops, Lucas drew in a breath of smoke-filled air and finally remembered his original objective. Saving Teal.

"Show me the right hole to reach the woman," Lucas demanded as he flew.

The owl turned a spiteful, evil grin in his direction and narrowed his beady, yellow eyes. *"Foolish human. The thing you most despise is what you have become.*

*"You who wished to belong with the others have dared to change forms. Your Brotherhood and family will shun you as a witch. You wanted to belong? Now you do. You belong with us, Skinwalker."*

"No!" The pain of realization hit Lucas hard. How could he have done something so unthinking? He'd let his fear for Teal and his fantasies overtake his entire upbringing. Everything he had ever learned about the Navajo Way told him changing forms was wrong. Yet given the opportunity, he'd jumped at it.

Anger, guilt and frustration swamped him with emotions he'd seldom experienced. He wanted to kill the Skinwalker owl who'd tricked him.

Doing a barrel roll in the sky, Lucas turned, determined to do real damage to the owl. But as a more experienced flyer, the owl ducked, flew low and disappeared from Lucas's limited view.

Now what?

His anger evaporated with the owl's disappearance. But the overwhelming guilt remained. He desperately wanted to change back to human form, save Teal and then begin repenting his unfortunate choices for the rest of his life. Was he instead destined to spend that life as a Skinwalker?

Teal inched out of the narrow opening and fell on her knees in the twilight. Gasping the clean fresh air, she thanked whatever lucky star she was under for saving her life.

She'd made it out of the mine. Thank heaven.

For what had seemed like hours, she'd followed the cavern walls, moving uphill and always staying to the right. The last narrow passageway had been a tight squeeze, but then she had seen the dim light at the end of the shaft and pure determination had carried her all the way outside.

Alive. And safe.

Sitting back on her heels, Teal tried to gather her senses. Where was she? And could she find Lucas's location from here?

It had seemed to her that she'd traveled miles underground away from the deadly fire and the caved-in mine entrance. But within the confines of the dark and soundless cavern, she could've been traveling in circles for all she knew.

Her throat was still sore from the smoke and she badly needed a drink of water. There would be no calling out for help from her for a while. And her cell phone still had no signal bars out here in the desert.

Maybe she could figure out where she was by the stars. She had learned a little celestial navigation in survival training. But when she looked up, she discovered the skies above her had turned gray with intermittent cloud cover. No moon and few stars. No help from that direction.

In a few moments, she found herself getting cold and wrapped her arms around her body in a tight hug. As dank and chilly as it had been inside the cavern, outside here in the dusk of this high desert, the night air was becoming downright frigid.

Coughing, laughing and crying all at the same time, Teal murmured, "Lucas, where are you? I need you."

*"The man who protects you has committed a grave error."*

She stood and twirled around, looking for the man behind the low bass voice. "Who are you? *Where* are you?"

*"I am known as* Accipiter striatus, *Bright Eyes. I am of the Sharp-Shinned Hawk Clan, born for the Bird People. We are your saviors."*

"Oh. My. God." Teal raised her hands to her temples and squeezed her eyes shut.

A big bird was sitting about five feet away on a low sage branch…and talking to her! Had she lost consciousness? Or had her brain been so deprived of oxygen in the smoky mine shaft that she was hallucinating.

This could not be happening.

With her eyes closed, she didn't hear anything for a few moments so she decided to sneak her eyes open for a peak. Perhaps this was just a terrible dream after all.

*"We should hurry. The one who speaks to us needs you."*

Reality blurred, then vanished as Teal stood staring at the hawk who was addressing her in a formal manner. What had he been saying? In a moment, she overcame her fear and settled into a good case of the jitters.

This...uh...bird was talking about Lucas.

"What's wrong with him?" she sputtered. "Was he injured in the explosion or cave-in?"

*"The man has allowed himself to be tricked. We are now protecting him from harm, but every minute brings him closer to destruction."*

"Tricked? How? By whom?"

*"The Navajo witch came to him and offered a chance to become one with them. It is against nature's way. The man should not have accepted."*

"Witches? Oh, you mean the Skinwalkers." Panic and fear for Lucas tumbled through her in a much worse case of near-hysteria than she'd had for her own safety.

"What have they done to him? Tell me," she demanded.

*"We chased off the intruder, but the man has been left behind in the form of the evil one. He seems to be our clan brother, but he is not."*

"He's in bird form? But why? Why would he do such a thing?" Teal was more than confused.

Lucas had changed over? It was really, truly possible? And she had been so smug and sure such things were simply naive superstitions.

*"He tells us he thought to save you. He did not trust us, his allies, to do the job."*

He'd wanted to save her and allowed the Skinwalkers to trick him. *Oh, Lucas.*

"But what can I do? I don't know how to change him back if he can't do it for himself."

*"His arrogance in making the change has left him with no memory of the Brotherhood chants. His brothers have arrived at the mine but do not recognize their own."*

"You think I could talk to him, then. Translate his words for the Brotherhood?"

*"You are his only hope. But we must hurry. The longer he stays in unnatural form, the less chance he will have to return."*

"How far is it? Will it take us long to reach him?"

*"Not long, Bright Eyes. We will lead."*

Teal pulled out her cell phone and checked the status bars. Nothing yet.

In a few minutes it would be pitch dark except for a couple of stars that appeared every time the cloud cover broke. So she turned on her flashlight beam and prepared to make her way through the sand and boulders to find the man she'd left behind—the man who had been protecting her back.

She only hoped it wouldn't be too late to help him.

## Chapter 12

Lucas ducked behind a boulder downhill from the mine entrance. The Brotherhood had arrived and were setting up floodlights and searching for him.

But there was nothing he could do to make them understand his current predicament. His words would be lost in a flutter of wings and the sound of birdcalls.

He wanted to curse at them. They were too late. Their help was useless to him now. Instead, he eased down into a crack at the base of the boulder and hid, afraid of noises from the dry brush around him.

The Bird People were guarding him from the skies. But that wouldn't shield him from the many dangers that awaited him on the ground. Snakes, in particular, were a disaster just waiting to happen. But it was the nature of a burrowing owl to nest under the rocks and sand, not high in a tree above the rattlesnakes and other animal predators.

Trying to rediscover his true spirit, Lucas fought the urges of the evil ones. The longer he stayed in this form, the angrier and greedier he became. He felt there was no hope to overcome the Skinwalker forces coursing through him.

Why shouldn't he simply remain a bird? He liked soaring above the trees. He'd been dreaming of this for longer than he'd been dreaming of Teal.

And speaking of her, this would be a perfect excuse to leave her behind. To get her out of his thoughts once and for all. After all, she didn't understand their connection and would be leaving him in the end anyhow.

Yes. Finally freedom from the invisible tether that had tied him to visions of Teal for most of his life. It would be a huge relief. Freedom. Freedom to soar. Freedom from dreams and from the Brotherhood.

Exactly what did he mean to his Navajo cousins in the Brotherhood anyway? They who had teased and shunned him as a child. They had turned him into a freak sideshow when they needed him to become the "sensitive" for the Brotherhood. He owed them no real allegiance.

The longer he listened to Kody and Hunter Long calling out his name, the more bitter he became. They were the blood brothers of the Brotherhood. True clansmen with the same mother, who had no room in their lives for a man with no parents and whose only talents were artistic.

He was not a fighter and had never done battle. They didn't really respect him.

Growing ever more furious now, he tried to think of ways that a bird could get even with humans. Perhaps he would contact the Skinwalkers and make a deal.

A rustling noise sounded off to his left and sent an alarm through his body. Was it a predator? Could he fly away in time?

Through the soft night air, Lucas heard a woman's voice whispering his name. Teal.

"Lucas. It's me. I can understand your words, so please answer me."

He didn't want her to see him like this. It was bad enough that he hadn't found a way of protecting her from Skinwalker evil. Now he couldn't even help himself.

"The Bird People told me what happened," Teal said. "Let me help you. I can translate."

Lucas was torn. A big part of him wanted to stay hidden and skip seeing the scorn in her eyes when she looked at him in the form of a Skinwalker.

But this was his Teal. Just looking at her reminded him of all that she meant to him. What had he been thinking before when he'd wanted his freedom?

She was his everything. All balanced in black and white, she shone brightly even when he kept edging over into the gray.

Another huge part of him couldn't bear taking the risk of losing her for good just yet. Never being able to hold her in his arms again. Never…saying goodbye.

Trying to keep his voice from carrying the sudden spurt of fear mixed with sorrow that he'd felt, Lucas hopped out of the boulder's shadow and spoke to her. "I'm here. But I'm not sure what you can do."

"Oh, Lucas," she said with pity in her voice. "Don't you know I would do whatever it takes to help you? You allowed yourself to be tricked trying to save me. I have to do what I can for you in return."

He couldn't stand the look on her face. The combination of sympathy and repulsion was something he'd never thought he would see stamped across her beautiful features.

Teal knelt beside him. "Please. Let me tell the Brotherhood what's happened. The Bird People say your cousins know a chant that'll bring you back. But we have to hurry. Your time is running out."

"They may not want to help me. What I've done is too big a mistake."

"Don't say that. The Brotherhood is honorable and loyal. They won't desert you. I know they'll help."

If it had been anyone else in the universe begging him to help himself, Lucas would've turned them down and let embarrassment and guilt ruin his life. But because it was Teal, he agreed to go up the hill with her to confront his cousins.

Kody and Hunter began a series of chants that Lucas thought he should remember but couldn't place. Standing his ground before them, he watched for signs of condemnation in their eyes. But he didn't see the scorn he'd expected. He saw sympathy and some pity, and something suspiciously like real concern.

Lucas wasn't entirely sure that he appreciated the Brotherhood's bringing him back. For what? To face the loss of his medicine man status? Or to become known as a former Brotherhood member?

He wanted to shout at them that if it hadn't been for Teal, he would've gladly remained the way he was. But he refused to add to his own misery by telling anyone that he'd considered staying in the form of a bird.

Twenty minutes later Lucas was once again in human form, with a Navajo blanket covering his foolish naked body. The wickedness and anger were only now beginning to release their hold on him. At this point he just felt tired. Exhausted in both body and mind.

"You need a Ghost Way branch of the Evilway ceremony done on your behalf, Cousin," Hunter told him. "Let me drive you home while my brother arranges for clan members to come to your medicine hogan so we can begin the Sing soon."

"I can drive myself," Lucas told him. "The only thing I need is a good night's sleep. Then I'll be okay."

"Driving would be a very bad idea," Hunter said with a shake of his head. He turned to Teal for assistance in convincing his cousin. "Don't you agree with me, Special Agent?"

"I don't know much about Navajo traditions, and a ceremony called 'Ghost Way' certainly has an odd ring to it," she said by way of an answer. "But I do agree that Lucas needs to find his balance again before he can go back to the way he was.

"However," she added in a strong voice. "I'll be the one to drive him home."

Hunter stared at her for a long few seconds, then

gave a sharp nod of his head. "Very well. But expect the Brotherhood to show up on his doorstep within twenty-four hours to perform the proper ceremony. Neither his cousins nor the Dineh can afford to lose him to the Evil."

Without the sun or the moon to light the roads, Teal knew she'd be lost on the reservation, so Kody drove ahead in his pickup and she followed in Lucas's SUV all the way back to the house. Then Kody helped Lucas into his own big brass bed for the night while she waited outside in the hall.

"You'll be able to stay here with him tonight, won't you?" Kody asked once he was back outside the bedroom with the door closed.

"I won't leave. I've been living here in his guest bedroom for the last week anyway."

Kody studied her in the soft night-light of the hallway before he spoke again. "Whether you admit it to yourself or not, Teal, this has been as much a trauma for you as for my cousin. I know you appear physically well and have no lasting after effects from the cave-in and fire. But right now I'm more concerned about your emotional well-being.

"Seeing a human switch form and become a bird can't be easy for an outsider to handle," he continued. "Especially if that human is someone you care about. I'm sorry you had to become involved in our Skin-walker war."

"I haven't had much time to think it all over," she said with a shake of her head. "Though I'm sure I'll be fine in the long run. Don't worry about me. But you could do me a favor."

"Anything."

"Let my supervisor Chris know I'll be taking a couple of days leave. I want to stick around here until I'm sure Lucas is back to normal."

"I'll make the proper excuses for you," Kody told her. "But…"

"What?"

"I can tell from the look in your eyes that you're trying to find your own balance. I'm fairly sure you've lived your life up to now being ruled by Anglo laws. And you've been hiding behind your badge because you liked the structure it provided. I've been where you are.

"But you can't hide from your Navajo side any longer," he went on. "You'll have to come to terms with it. From now on you'll have to stop letting only the things you can prove be the guiding force of your life. There are other possibilities that must be acknowledged and accepted."

Teal didn't really want to talk about it. If given a choice, she didn't even want to think about such things. Not yet. Right this minute, Lucas had to be her main focus.

She thanked Kody for all his help, agreed to attend Lucas's curing ceremony they had scheduled for tomorrow afternoon, and then waited until she heard Kody drive away before she went back to the hall outside Lucas's door and settled down.

A noise must've disturbed her sleep. Teal woke up and looked around, wondering what time it was. She hadn't been asleep for too long, she knew. She'd sat in the hall, listening for Lucas to make a noise until the wee hours of the morning. But as she looked outside her window now, darkness still ruled.

Part of her fully expected to see Skinwalkers jumping from behind every shadow. The other part wanted something to happen, either good or bad, so she would have something to do. Some chore to fulfill. Something to keep her busy.

This hanging out and wringing her hands was so not her style. But the quiet of the dead of night and the lack of sounds from Lucas's bedroom had given her nothing to do but worry. At about 2:00 a.m. she'd decided to slip into her own bed for a few hours sleep.

Now something had just awoken her from that sleep. She checked the lighted dial on the clock and saw it was four-thirty. Not even dawn yet. She'd only been in bed for a couple of hours.

When her eyes adjusted to the dark, she eased out of bed and went to find out what had awakened her. Was something or someone trying to break into the house? Lucas had told her when she came to live here that this house had been specially blessed. Evil couldn't get in.

But she wasn't quite as positive as he'd been. After all, the evil he'd recently overcome had shown several faces. Some of those evil faces appeared quite capable of getting past all obstacles to get what they wanted, too.

In a few moments she discovered his bedroom door stood wide open and Lucas's bed was empty. Had someone come in and kidnapped him?

Making a silent dash back to her bedroom, Teal grabbed her weapon from under the pillow. She checked it, then picked up a flashlight. Whatever had happened to Lucas, it would be better if she stayed quiet and kept the lights off until she knew what she would be facing.

She crept through the house, listening intently for any noise. Checking the doors and windows as she went, Teal found everything just as she'd left it.

Upon entering the kitchen, she heard another noise. This time it was clearly coming from Lucas's studio on the other side of the narrow hallway.

Was someone stealing artwork or jewelry? If so, where was Lucas? She hoped like crazy that he was not about to do something stupid. He was too weakened by all that had happened in the last twenty-four hours to try apprehending a burglar. Even though that would be typical of something he might be tempted to do.

Teal flattened herself against the solid wall at the back of the studio and let her eyes adjust to shadows created by the outside lights streaming through the floor-to-ceiling windows at the far end of the room. She saw something move down there and narrowed her eyes trying to see what it was.

The breath caught in her throat when she finally spotted him. Lucas. Standing there, naked except for a pair of nylon running shorts, with his hands on his hips and staring out the window.

The full force of his masculinity hit her smack in the gut. His body was lean and taut. His muscles quivering with energy.

The man had literally stolen her breath away.

Suddenly, a picture of the two of them tangled in each other's embrace budded in her mind. She shifted uncomfortably inside her sweat suit.

Why hadn't the two of them had sex yet? They'd been living under the same roof for days. And every time she looked into his eyes, the depth of his desire was clear.

So why not? Had she subconsciously put up barriers between them the way she had done with others for most of her life?

What a load of crap. She was a confident and intelligent woman who knew her own worth. Why had she been such a cold fish in the past? Was she frigid?

As the sweat trickled down between her breasts, she realized the way she felt now was decidedly not cold. Nor did she have any wish to continue being only a buddy and a pal—at least not with this man.

Okay, so the two times before Lucas that she'd tried having a sexual encounter had been less than noteworthy. But maybe those times had not really been all her fault.

She had the distinct impression that right now she was finally about to encounter her own passion. Big-time.

Quietly she lowered her weapon and the flashlight, and laid them on a corner of Lucas's drafting table.

But then she hesitated. Would coming on to him tonight be fair?

He was a wounded soul. A man trying to recapture his spirit. Perhaps another time would be more appropriate.

Trying hard to conquer her body's growing needs, Teal took a slow, uneasy breath. Perhaps a little too loudly.

Lucas's head whipped around, his gaze snapped up her body and met her eyes. She knew right away that this night was going to be fine with him, too.

The need was there in his eyes, overpowering any hesitation and whatever emotional turmoil he'd been going through. He wanted her. And judging by the look and the growing tightness in his muscles, even more desperately than she'd wanted him.

He came toward her then. Silently stalking across the room, his gaze never faltered. She could sense him watching her breathe, even through the darkness. Felt his stare as if it was a bold caress.

She suddenly imagined him as the hunter and herself as the prey. Not a totally uncomfortable feeling for some reason. But also not exactly as she had envisioned.

It seemed to take him forever to reach her. And the growing frenzy inside her body had already made her wet with the wait.

By the time he was within reach, she was nearly giddy with desire. She bit down on her lip—and held still.

Lucas's heart was pounding, the blood rushing through his veins—and heading straight to his groin. The way she was looking at him, as if she *knew*. Knew with certainty about the dreams. It was too much. Too much need.

Every time he'd closed his eyes over the last few days, he had remembered. And hungered.

Whenever they were together, the force between their bodies shimmered with power and static electricity, even in the worst of times — those hard times when he'd had to fight his base instincts and reject both greed and anger.

Yet she had remained by his side. Stood by him as only a mate would do. Even now, she lifted her chin slightly, the female animal's sign of readiness.

He found himself clenching and unclenching his fists, wanting to drive deep into the welcoming warmth he'd found in his dreams. Instead he decided to take it slow and easy. He didn't wish to frighten her by coming on too strong. She might not have the same memories as he did.

Almost afraid to move, Lucas gently lifted a hand to cup her face. Soft and smooth and warm to the touch, her skin caused an even wilder combustion to explode inside him. She rested her cheek in his palm as if there was nowhere else on earth she would rather be.

He bent to brush her lips with his own. Just a touch. Nothing too threatening.

But as he began to pull away, she surprised him by reaching up and grabbing the sides of his head. Dragging him down closer to her once again, Teal appeared reluctant to rush yet determined not to move back.

Their lips were but a whisper apart. Her scent drifted to his nostrils and captured whatever sanity he had left. This was the part that had been missing from his dreams. The musky, womanly smell of her invading his senses, seeping inside every pore.

He remembered the things she had liked and disliked from his dreams. But now the reality stumped him. She was like a brand-new puzzle with millions of pieces he needed to fit together to make the whole of what was Teal.

Teal felt his hesitation and fought the urge to speed up his reactions. She was sure she could do it. Sure she could touch him in just the right way with her hands and her mouth in order to make him crazy with desire.

But that wasn't the way she wanted things to go. Not this time.

Ready to lead the way slowly, she wanted to drag it out. To feel every touch of lips and fingers. To memorize all the moves and sensations that came with them. This was their time. And she was determined to make the most of it for however long she could.

At last she touched her lips to his. He moaned, deep and low with a guttural tone, and opened his mouth to invite her in. Starting slowly, she swirled her tongue into his mouth to create a rhythm. Moving as if she was painting his tongue with her own, she dipped and laved and sucked. Then she mixed up the action by nibbling on his lower lip.

The heat was building between them, heading toward something explosive though they'd hardly even laid a hand on each other. Teal remembered to breathe deeply, trying not hurry. But as she inhaled, the sexual energy from their touching lips spread all over her body.

Hell. She was driving herself nuts with all this touching but not touching.

Desperate to slow down, she tried visualizing her inner being—the parts of her that had always been empty and in need of filling up.

She wanted Lucas to be the one to fill them—slowly and with feeling. But she wasn't sure either one of them would last long enough to make it good.

Well, if this time was destined to be over in a hurry, Teal decided to make the most of it. She stepped back, pulled her sweatshirt over her head and shimmied out of her sweatpants and panties at the same time.

Lucas's nostrils flared at the sight of her naked body before him. His pupils darkened as he reached out for her. It was plain that he was as ready as she was.

In one fell swoop, he stepped out of his shorts and dragged her to his chest. The friction of his body against hers drove pinpricks of sensation between her legs.

She was definitely ready. "Let's head for your bed," she groaned, trying to make it last a few minutes more.

"In the bed, in the shower, on the kitchen counter. Anywhere you like," he whispered as his hands found her bottom and pressed her damp spot against his erection. "But later. Right now, it's here. Right here. Right now."

Not really wanting to protest, Teal leaned into him. He found her mouth again with a searing kiss. It was a deep spirit-melding kiss, backed by all the desperation they both were feeling. Lucas lifted her off her feet without breaking the kiss. She automatically wound her legs around his waist and hung on.

Teal was lost in sensation as his arousal probed her hot center. Her good intentions evaporated, and she just had to feel him inside her. Now.

Lucas leaned his back against the wall to steady himself, and the movement of his hips drove his tip just inside her. She went wild with desire.

"Now," she demanded. "Please, now." Her insides were clutching.

He growled, with a low and feral sound that drove her to an even higher frenzy. "Anything you want, Bright Eyes."

She wanted to hold on, to make it last. But the instant he pushed himself inside her, she already felt the fireworks begin.

*Oh, Lucas.*

## Chapter 13

Sparks shot down her spine as Teal felt him go over the edge with her. He jerked and moaned in tandem with her scream. Then for moments there was no sight nor sound except for the fingers of fire that consumed her.

Holding her close, he kissed the top of her head and her temples. Lucas seemed to be regulating his breathing just as her own was leveling out. She gulped and released her grip on him.

He let her slide down his body until her feet were back on the ground. "You okay, Bright Eyes?" He ducked his head to see her face, but he didn't let her out of his embrace.

"The best."

"That wasn't too…"

"It was. It was too good, too everything. But now it's too damned over. Can we do it again?" she asked and flashed him a smile.

"Ah." The grin on his face was full of self-satisfaction and masculine pride. "I think by the time we reach my bed I'll be ready to slow it down the next time."

"Oh, you…" She pushed at his biceps and giggled like a schoolgirl. "It was a long day. For both of us. You need your sleep." She pulled totally out of his arms and turned away.

He grabbed her wrist, swung her back around and against his chest. "I need *you* more."

Teal barely got out a squeak before he picked her up in his arms and headed through the kitchen toward his bedroom.

"You want a drink of water?" he asked as he passed the sink.

But he didn't let her answer. Instead he covered her mouth with a fiery, grazing kiss. The blast of heat his kiss caused began in her chest and quickly moved to all the feminine parts that had not yet quit pulsating from their last encounter.

"No water, thanks," she mumbled when he lifted his head at last.

"Hungry?"

"Uh… That depends on what you have in mind."

He laughed, and it was the best sound she'd heard in days. Without another word, he carried her to his room and deposited her on the bed.

Standing over her, he gazed down at her naked body with a wicked leer. "I want to make you crazy for me."

"I already am." She lifted her arms up in invitation.

Lucas folded his arms across his bare chest and stayed where he was, complete with a silly smile plastered on his face.

"Really, I am," she said, as she noticed the whine that had crept into her voice. "Certifiably crazy. Nuts. Wacko. Totally overboard. Isn't that good enough?"

Tumbling onto the bed with a chuckle, he wrapped her body in his arms and rolled. Within a moment, they both lay sprawled and laughing. Him on the bottom on his back and her splayed out across his chest.

"Ah, that's better." He palmed her buttocks and squeezed.

Teal gave in to the sensual mood he'd created. She'd been wanting the two of them in this bed in the first place. Had been thinking about it ever since the moment she spotted the big brass headboard.

Inching upward, she captured his mouth with a hot kiss. "I like having you where I want you," she told him when she lifted her head. "This is exactly right."

"Oh yeah? And what do you have in mind to do with me?"

She opened her knees, planted them on either side of his waist and sat up, straddling him. "Lots of things," she whispered as she rubbed her hands across his chest. "Good things." She wanted him to feel good. Be happy. And to forget all that had happened to him at the mine.

His eyes widened and darkened and the smile on his

lips turned slightly dangerous. He reached up and used his fingers to flirt with her nipples. Rolling, pinching, then massaging.

"I have dreamed of this a thousand times, Bright Eyes. Just this." He bent in two and laved one sensitive tip, nipping it with his teeth.

"Oh. Oh…"

This wasn't altogether what she had in mind. She'd wanted to drive him as crazy as she was. But at this rate she'd completely stop thinking any moment now and be totally useless.

"No fair. It's my turn." She flashed him as flirty a smile as she knew how to give, then hitched in a breath and flipped herself, straddling him again with her back to his sexy grin.

Here was a much better position for what she had in mind. This way she had full access to his erection and he couldn't distract her.

She ran a fingertip up his fullness to the moist tip and listened to him moan. Laughing aloud and reveling in the moment, she was thrilled to have him under her power.

"Teal…"

As he said her name on a whispered breath, Teal's mind flashed on a half-remembered dream. A shadow of an emotion. A time out of time.

She'd been here before. Right here on his big brass bed, teasing him. This man she'd thought was a stranger had appeared to her in the shadows of the night many years ago.

When exactly? And how? She didn't really want to

know. She'd always thought that dreams were her enemy, and hated every one she'd ever had. Just like the one she'd had during her first night here. Nasty. Ugly things.

She wanted to bury every image. They were all too gray and hazy for a woman who needed things to be in black and white.

So why did she seem to be flashing on an old dream scene right now? She refused to go there, no matter that it might have included Lucas and probably sex. Tonight, she'd deliberately act differently from anything that might've been in any dream. She decided to make new memories. Real ones.

Shaking her head, she ripped at the braid in her hair and set the long, black mass free. This was no dream. It was real and he was real. And she was determined to live through every single live emotion.

She could do this.

Lucas had been laughing along with the sexy woman of his dreams who straddled him. He enjoyed her taking the reins. She was exquisite in her lust.

But suddenly something had seemed to change for her. The atmosphere, or the musk in the night. Whatever it was, Teal quit giggling and was holding perfectly still.

When she'd let her long silky hair loose, it had whipped around her back and he had images of burying his hands in it. Of letting the soft strands slide through his fingers as he held her head still for a kiss.

With this quiet, he wasn't sure of anything. It was

quite a different scenario than in any of his dreams. But Lucas didn't care a bit. She was still his dream girl.

He held his breath waiting for her. In a moment she lifted up on her knees and hovered over him.

His hands went to her hips and he helped guide her down on him. As he filled her, Lucas heard her moan—a low, keening sound that ran along his nerve endings and made him go wild with desire.

Running his hands up her sides and then along her spine, he could feel her trembling under his fingertips. He began to move his hips.

"Stop it. Not that way," she cried.

He froze. "Am I hurting you?"

"No. No. It's just… It's my turn. I'll do it differently this time."

Lucas had no idea what she'd meant by that, but he had her exactly where he wanted her—in his bed. And he wasn't about to ruin it by doing anything she didn't want.

She sighed, then hiccuped a tiny sob. Something was definitely not right with her.

"Teal. Stop now. Let me just hold you for a while."

He wanted to see her face. Had to know what she was feeling. He couldn't tell a thing with her back to him.

She gasped, "No. I'm fine."

Lifting her bottom again, she let herself back down, slow and easy. It felt wonderful, but Lucas was still worried about her.

This had never happened in any of his many dreams. Teal had always been wild and wanton. Never silent, never hesitant. In fact, just a few minutes ago in his studio she'd let herself go. She'd been hot and desperate and so ready that she'd exploded at the very first thrust.

He didn't necessarily need her to be that wild. Soft and slow was every bit as erotic to him. But he didn't want her unhappy. Not ever.

Leaning back, she took him to the hilt. Her long hair streamed over him and tickled his chest. With the tight and welcoming fit of her, he felt as if he'd finally arrived back where he belonged.

Lucas lifted his back off the bed and wrapped his arms around her. He would hold her safe and warm and let her make all the moves she wanted.

She gasped again and tried to sit up. He lifted, with her still in his arms, until they both were sitting up. Spooned together that way, she began to move once more.

He scraped a thumb over her nipple and put his mouth on the back of her neck. She cried out and moved in earnest.

Suddenly things were all fast and furious, raw and savage. Heat mixed with electric impulses. It was as if he'd put a match to dynamite.

Feeling her coming undone around him, Lucas let himself go. Waves of pleasure ripped through her into him until they both cried out with the intensity.

He wanted to howl, to shout, to cry.

Instead, he pulled her down to the bed, tucked her in to lie next to him and wrapped her in his embrace.

This had been the most sensual thing that had ever happened to him.

Holding her close and listening as her breathing evened out, he wondered how many more times they had remaining before she left him for good. And what he would ever do without her after tonight?

Could he go back to having her only as a dream girl?

* * *

Teal rolled over and opened one sleepy eye. Light streamed in around closed blinds in Lucas's bedroom. It must be late.

She turned and went right back to the snuggly warm spot she'd been occupying under Lucas's arm. Who cared if it was past daybreak—or even if it was past noon?

There was no need for either of them to get up yet. His curing ceremony would not begin for hours yet, and she had taken a few days off.

Closing her eyes again, Teal smiled to herself. What a wonderful night it had been. They had reached for each other over and over. What she remembered the most was a powerful pounding in her ears. A hammering of blood and heat and heart.

As she lay there feeling her body come awake with its memories of pleasure, Teal also noticed a subtle shift in her feelings. In the cave yesterday she'd discovered that she'd grown to like Lucas a lot. And she had wanted to save him when things looked bad. Then of course, she'd been wanting to have sex with him—

desperately—ever since she'd first seen him on that ledge in Many Caves Canyon.

But there was something else. Something new. Something more.

Thinking about how she felt, she curled up and soaked in his body heat as she listened to him softly snoring. What was the difference now?

She could remember from last night a powerful urge to keep him safe and happy. Happy? Yes. She needed him to be happy more than she wanted happiness for herself.

Her throat went dry. Never before had someone else's well-being meant more than her own. Hell.

Tears began to gather at the back of her eyes. But they weren't tears of joy. They weren't even tears of misery.

As they leaked from the corners of her eyes, Teal realized the tears on her cheeks were for him. For Lucas. He'd lived through so much in his lifetime. Then she'd arrived on the scene and caused him even more grief. Most of the bad things that had happened to him recently were because of her.

That wasn't something she wanted to dwell on. Not now while she was curled up against his side and basking in the goodness of their lovemaking. Maybe after his ceremony when he was once again well, she would talk to him about all that had happened—now and in her dreams.

Lucas sat naked on a log inside the tarp of his sweat lodge, tending to the fire. The north wind was kicking

up outside and bringing the first real bluster of winter
to the Lukachukai Mountains.

He'd hated leaving Teal to her own devices back
inside his house—especially after last night. But a big
part of the ceremony he would undergo later today was
dependent upon him taking a sweat bath in preparation.

Rubbing his eyelids with the back of his knuckles,
Lucas tried to clear his mind. It didn't seem worthwhile
thinking about Teal. That way led to confusion and potential sorrow. Not to clarity. Not to harmony and
balance.

The kindling he'd gathered earlier was beginning to
catch and flames crackled warmly before him. He'd
placed his rocks in the proper formation, and had a
bucket of clean, fresh water standing by. Now he sat
with his legs crossed, waiting for the fire to burn itself
down to coals. The rocks needed to get hot enough.

Trying not to think of Teal and how he felt about
the reality of the woman he had loved in his dreams,
Lucas turned his thoughts instead to the reason for his
upcoming Sing.

All by itself, the matter of his talking to a Skinwalker would've been enough for him to need a cure.
But becoming one of them— That was not anything
the Brotherhood had ever faced.

A year or so ago, they'd helped those teenager
athletes who had fallen prey to Skinwalker promises
of money and fame. The Brotherhood had found a
healing cure for them then. In fact, that particular Sing,
along with a little psychic hypnosis, had cured both the

young men and the young nurse who had been so confused and tricked by her Skinwalker boyfriend.

But Lucas wasn't so sure that the same cure would work for him. His sensitive's mind would not allow him to be cured by any hypnosis.

How had he gotten himself in such a fix?

He thought about how he'd felt soaring along the downdrafts. He thought about the unusual, and terrible anger that had run through his being. He thought about the Burrowing Owl Skinwalker, whose thoughts had seeped into his subconscious mind.

What? Did he really have buried memories of what the Skinwalker had been thinking? If so, he needed to remember. Perhaps his thoughts could lead the Brotherhood to the Owl or his witch brothers.

The fire had burned itself down to coals by now. Lucas squatted before it and reveled in the hot, dry air. Like a sauna, the warm heat had begun the body cleansing he so needed. Sweat trickled down his neck as perspiration soaked through every pore.

Singing sweat chants the ancients had taught to the People centuries ago, he relaxed his muscles and let the sickness and evil seep from his body. In a few minutes he dipped his hand into the bucket of water and sprinkled droplets onto the rocks. Steam sizzled off the fiery basalt and surrounded him in moisture.

Soon he was engulfed in a hazy, stifling fog. Images began to swirl before his eyes. He lifted a hand to his forehead and swiped away the sweat, then rested back on his haunches.

A movie began playing out in his head. A movie

starring a wild, yellow-eyed wolf. The Navajo Wolf. The half man, half witch who'd ruled the dark forces in Dinetah over the last few years.

Lucas suddenly knew the man's evil power. It was seductive and tantalizing, though somewhere underneath it all, he could feel the Wolf losing strength. There was something not quite right in the Skinwalker's world. Lucas sensed a growing panic and insanity in the man who became the Wolf.

Shaking his head in order to peer through the mist, it began to feel as if Lucas was seeing things through the eyes of a timid, half burrowing owl. One who longed to usurp the Wolf's reign. The Owl was lying back and waiting for his chance. Waiting and watching for the moment when he could rise up and dominate the evil armies all on his own.

Without losing his focus, Lucas dropped more water against the rocks. Taking a deep, cleansing breath, he waited for the visions to continue.

*"Our operations are going well, Owl."* The Wolf *was in the form of a man with a pocked face and longish animal-like snout. "Killing that tribal spy for no good reason was an excellent idea. Senseless evil and diversion will send our enemies reeling. The FBI and the Brotherhood will be chasing their tails, giving us enough time to continue our search for the map.*

*"My map. They have no right to that map. It guides the way to Skinwalker secrets. It's nothing fit for mere humans to see."*

Lucas felt a chill climbing up the spine of the Owl

whose head he was occupying. He heard himself telling the Wolf whatever he wanted to hear.

*"Yes, sirrrr..."* he stuttered. *"Already, more and more of the Brotherhood have quit searching for the map as they gather to assist their own.*

*"You would've had a good laugh when the woman FBI agent interrogated foolish environmentalists who only wanted peaceful protest. Our enemies spin their wheels, going in opposing directions."*

*The Wolf wheezed in a breath and grabbed the Owl by the scruff of the neck. "I laugh at nothing until the parchments are in my hands. The woman means nothing. Kill her if necessary. But bring me that map, you idiot."*

Lucas jerked his head and snapped out of the foggy haze of images surrounding him. Relief poured over him like the beads of moisture glistening on his skin from the failing steam. He was back.

Inhaling deeply, he felt dizzy now. But at least he was in his own head and his own time. Free once again from the grisly anger—and the spine-tingling fear.

With each breath, he relished his health and good genes. He tested the strong calf muscles he had honed and trained. He rejoiced in the vigor in his lungs and the power in his shoulders, reminding him that he was human and Navajo.

His physical well-being was his *hozho*, his balance. It took losing it to an owl to make him appreciate his health.

Going with the flow of life was the Navajo Way. If you can't win the battle, learn to make a friend of your

enemy—but watch him closely. Above all, keep your
harmony and balance.

When he emerged from the sweat lodge, Lucas
knew what was he was destined to do. He grabbed a
towel and headed for the shower.

"What do you mean the curing ceremony is off?
Why? I thought everyone was coming here. I
thought..." Teal was astonished and nearly speechless
as Lucas shrugged a shoulder and looked away.

She'd found him outside here under the cottonwoods, bending over small piles of different-colored
sands. He had been chanting softly to himself and
sifting handfuls of the sand in his palm one at a time.

He didn't look up. "I called everyone and told them
not to come. It took some fast-talking to convince the
Brotherhood that I know what I'm doing. I don't need
them and they are needed elsewhere more."

What was he talking about?

She crouched down beside him. "Tell me what's
happened. What's wrong?"

"Have I ever told you about the sand painting?" he
asked. "About how wonderful it is to be able to make
a good living doing something so sacred—and
helpful?"

He wanted to discuss sand painting. Now?

She stood up and stared at him. His hair was still
damp from a shower. His soft jeans and flannel shirt
looked terribly romantic today. His long artistic
fingers, the style of his thick black hair growing over

# Chapter 14

Teal stood over him, glaring down at the sand he'd been sifting. "You've never mentioned your sand painting, except to point them out on your walls." She lifted her chin and looked around. "Have you seen Snow lately, by the way? This sand looks like something he could really get into."

She graced him with a wry grin and Lucas's heart flipped over. His spirit was already crying at the coming loss of that haunting smile.

"Though the cat has the new special privilege of going outside with you, Snow has been imprisoned in the house temporarily," he told her. "That *bilagaana* cat cannot be allowed out when I'm working in sand."

Chuckling, Teal folded her arms over her chest. "So you're working? It doesn't look like you've gotten too much done. And this whole discussion still doesn't tell me why you changed your mind about the ceremony."

Lucas dribbled a few grains of sand out on the board below him. "Things change, Teal. Times change. Just like these grains of sand, sometimes life has to be rearranged.

"In the Navajo Way, medicine men use sacred sand paintings within their healing ceremonies," he added. "The sacred ones are not at all like the pieces of art you've seen throughout my house. Each Singer must ceremoniously destroy his sacred paintings, wipe them all away before dawn or risk taboos against both himself and his patient."

Lucas wondered if he could find a way to tell her about the dreams—before she left for good. He wasn't sure he had the nerve.

He needed to forget who he was. A man with a consuming need to be accepted. He wasn't sure her nontraditional upbringing would ever be able to accept that part of him.

It didn't matter about his needs at the moment, though. She was the reason for everything he was about to do.

Standing up beside her, he spilled the remaining sand back on the ground and took her hand. "We need to talk. Walk with me for a few minutes."

"Okay. But I still don't..."

"Have you ever seen me in a dream, Bright Eyes?" The question both interrupted and seemed to stun her.

"I don't dream."

"I know better. You had a nightmare the first night you stayed here with me." He took a few steps toward the cottonwoods and the nearly dry spring below them. "You might not remember them. But I remember all of mine."

"No, I..." Her face held a terrified expression as her voice seemed to give out on her.

"Don't worry. It's not that important," he said, trying to soothe her. "Just let me tell you one dream story.

"There once was a boy. A lonely boy of about eleven. He dreamed of a lonely girl, just about his same age. He dreamed they became friends in the night. Comrades in their loneliness."

She stopped walking and looked over at him, a fearful expression on her face. He hadn't wanted to upset her, only to explain.

"They were pals," he stated again more firmly. "The boy and girl met in almost every dream of his and became close friends. As he grew older, the girl grew, too—getting taller and more slender. Her firm breasts and long legs stirred new feelings in our lonely teenager. He began to hunger for her, the way a man hungers for a woman."

"I'm..." She cleared her throat and inched back into the shadow of the yellow cottonwood leaves. "I'm not sure I want to hear the rest of this. I feel like the story is turning into an Internet porno site."

"It might have been," he told her. "It very well *could* have been. Except that he and the girl had fallen for each other long before they consummated their mutual desire. By then he was desperately in love, after years of pouring out his heart to her, his only friend."

"But this was a dream," Teal said quickly. "It wasn't real life."

"That's exactly what our young man's wife told him," Lucas told her sadly. "You see, he'd thought so, too. Thought his nighttime lover was only a dream. In his real life he'd found himself a good woman, one who cared deeply about him. And he married her, hoping to forget the dream girl and start living life in the daylight."

"But he couldn't," Teal said in a tiny voice.

"No. Our hero couldn't shake the dreams. He began to see the dream girl in everything he did. When his wife sighed in the night, he pictured his lover. He couldn't get rid of the dream's tastes and textures. He ached for her—and dreamed of her."

"And the wife knew."

"She knew. But tried to forget. Soon, whatever love she'd had for him at first was gone. And within months, so was she."

"Oh, Lucas. That boy was you, wasn't it?"

He nodded. "And the dream girl—was you."

"No." Teal drew back. "It couldn't have been me. We've never met before... Before..."

Stepping close, he ran a finger softly down her cheek, following a single teardrop. "You know it's true. You've dreamed of me, too."

Teal shivered and began to tremble. "I don't want to talk about dreams anymore. And definitely not about mine. Get to the point. Why aren't you having that ceremony?"

"I had a vision this morning," he confessed. "Another kind of dream. I've discovered that I can still see and hear the Skinwalkers. I...I'm only one dream away from being in the Owl's thoughts, Bright Eyes.

"I can't be a Dineh medicine man like that," he went on, hurrying to get it all out. "I can't help the Brotherhood or myself. And I especially can't help you as long as the evil remains inside me."

"You don't mean that," she cried. "Isn't there something that can be done? Some ceremony. Surely the Brotherhood can..."

Lucas slipped his arm around her shoulders. "Shush. It's okay. I've already come to terms with not being able to help the Brotherhood anymore.

"Ever since you arrived, my dream girl, I haven't been able to read anyone's thoughts. My whole mission—my one real contribution to the Brotherhood—has disappeared."

Teal held in the gasp that had threatened to become a sob. She didn't want to hear any more. Things had been going wrong for Lucas ever since the moment she'd arrived. She'd had that very same thought just last night. But this? This was too terrible even to contemplate.

Had she ruined his entire life? First her image had cost him his wife. Had she taken away his hard-earned position of respect as a medicine man and Brotherhood warrior now, as well?

She twisted her shaky hands and tried not to think.

Just then, a voice called out from up near the house and suddenly everything changed once more.

* * *

*"Ya'at'eeh,"* Kody Long sang out as he got nearer.

Lucas returned the Navajo greeting, took Teal's hand and walked out into the hazy sunshine to meet his cousin. Teal was wondering what the FBI special agent was doing here in the middle of the day if there was to be no ceremony. She was having a weird premonition that something big was about to happen.

"Cousin," Kody said as he nodded to Lucas. "I have some news that concerns Special Agent Benaly. Well, for both of you."

Teal could tell that Lucas was holding his breath and waiting, the same way she was. He dropped her hand so she could shake Kody's.

"Has something bad happened?" Lucas asked.

"Not really. I attended a meeting a while ago with Chapter Councilman Ayze and Teal's boss, Special-Agent-In-Charge Sullivan. Councilman Ayze is well aware of what you two faced in that mine yesterday. He knows about the Brotherhood and is behind our efforts to eliminate the Skinwalkers."

Teal looked over at Lucas, but his expression revealed nothing. This was one of those times she wished she could read minds. Was that a grimace she saw behind his eyes?

"Chris doesn't know anything about this, does he?" she asked Kody.

"No. Our Skinwalker war is not something he can do anything about, so he does not have a need to know. It's a Dineh problem. Anglos have no federal laws that apply to this particular reservation tradition."

After he'd spoken those words, she noticed that Lucas nodded to him. The move was almost imperceptible, but she had noticed. Wondering what the look between them had meant, she turned her focus back to Kody.

"The Brotherhood made some…discreet inquiries this morning," Kody told her. "We've learned that the young Navajo man who was killed was a sacrifice of the Skinwalkers. There has never been any conspiracy among the environmental groups who have been demonstrating at the coal mines."

"A sacrifice? What does that mean?"

"Apparently, the Skinwalkers have been keeping close tabs on the Brotherhood. They knew we had leads to finding a map they lost. A map they want back badly. So they decided to detour us with creative diversions," Kody continued. "The arsons and accidents around the mines were all done by the Skinwalkers to get our attention. And the man who was Councilman Ayze's assistant unfortunately stepped into their way."

"That's awful," she murmured. "But I don't understand how that would sideline your war. The FBI is the agency that investigates murders on federal reservation land. After all, it wasn't any of you that was assigned to investigate, it was…" Her voice trailed off when she realized what she was saying.

She'd been used by the Skinwalkers as a pawn in their dangerous chess game with the Brotherhood. Dammit.

Kody threw Lucas a quick and indeterminate look. "You, Teal. Again, I'm sorry you got involved. And what's worse, the whole environmental point the Skin-walkers were using to their advantage no longer matters now."

"What? Why?"

"The owners of Black Mesa mine announced this morning they'll be shutting down. As of the first of the year, there will be no more coal-mining jobs there. Nor any reason to use our groundwater for a coal sluice that no longer runs. The power plant isn't making enough money for them, so it's going, too. The environmental groups are all disbanding or moving elsewhere."

"That's kind of 'good news, bad news' for the People, isn't it?"

"Yeah, it is. And unfortunately, it's the same kind of thing for you."

"Why me?" Teal was positive she wasn't going to be happy to hear Kody's next bit of news.

"You've been reassigned. Off the reservation. You're needed temporarily in the sub-agency field office in Durango. Actually, they need you there by the day after tomorrow."

Teal felt her knees go weak. Her job? She'd been reassigned. Demoted was more like it.

A few days ago that news would've killed her. Today, all she could think about was leaving the reservation. Leaving Lucas.

The tears welled in her eyes, but she battled them back. This had to be for the best. Hadn't she just been thinking about how bad her influence had been in Lucas's life?

"I see," she managed with an amazing calm in her voice. "Did Chris happen to tell you how I'm supposed to get to Durango? The motor pool still hasn't put my car back in order."

"I'll drive you tomorrow." Lucas stepped closer and spoke for the first time since Kody had arrived.

"Oh, there's no need for you to go out of your way." She couldn't imagine how hard it was going to be to say goodbye.

"Yes, I'm afraid there is," Kody broke in. "The Skinwalkers know who you are now. And they know hurting you can get us involved. You need a Brotherhood guard until you're safely off the reservation, and none of the rest of us are available. Lucas will deliver you to your new assignment."

For a moment it flashed in her head that she was being set up somehow. Had the Brotherhood gotten her demoted in order to protect her?

She refused to think that way. Look what havoc she'd already caused them. Her poor job performance was her own doing.

But this leaving business was too hard. She'd already ruined the life of the man she loved. And now she was forcing him to leave his home in order to get rid of her.

How could she?

"Fine," she told Kody without looking over at Lucas. "If you'll excuse me, I'll go pack."

She started toward the house, hesitated then turned back to Kody. "I want to thank you for helping me out while I was assigned here, Special Agent Long. It's

been a pleasure meeting you. Even under the circumstances."

He nodded to her. "You take care, Special Agent
Benaly. Maybe we'll run into each other again."

Goodbyes were too much for her to bear. She spun
around and ran back into the house before she made a
huge fool of herself and broke down into little-girly
tears.

That was so *not* what one-of-the-guys Benaly
would normally let anyone see her do.


"But why does your grandmother want to talk to
me?" she asked Lucas just as the orange streaks from
the setting sun electrified the sky to the west.

"She didn't tell me. But she wants you to come spend
your last night with her. I…agreed. It would be better if
we weren't together tonight. Being with you and
knowing it was our last night would be too hard on me,
Teal."

Too hard on him? Lord, how was she ever going to
live through the next twenty-four hours?

"She's not going to try to poison me again, is she?"

Lucas tsked at her, then smiled. "That's not
amusing," he said through his grin. "She cured you the
last time. And you must admit, you needed your rest
then. Didn't you heal faster after you saw her?"

"Well, all right. I'll go stay with her. The SUV's
already loaded with my stuff. I guess I'm ready. Shall
we walk over?"

"It'll be easier, if you don't mind."

They took off at an easy pace to walk the half mile

down the hill toward his grandmother's quaint hogan. There was a strained quiet between them, and Teal was relieved to be spending the night out of his house.

Within a few minutes, a gunmetal gray cloud passed right over their heads, and an intermittent, light sprinkle erupted right above them—just to make their walk harder.

"I don't believe I've ever seen it rain like this here on the rez."

"It's a female rain. Soft. The thunderstorms are male and can be dangerous."

"Right. Whatever you say."

A streak of black fur raced past her feet and disappeared into the scrub up the road. "What was that?"

"Snow. I believe he's decided to stay at my grandmother's hogan with you tonight. But he doesn't care much for the rain."

Teal had become friends with the Anglo cat and was glad he would keep her company tonight. She liked Lucas's grandmother, but the old woman made her a little nervous.

Looking out for Snow, she gazed up ahead toward the west and realized the skies there had become brilliant maroon, lit by the setting sun. They were walking through a crimson rain. Lucas's valley had all of a sudden turned into a magic fairyland on fire.

"Isn't it beautiful?" she asked with a sigh.

"Yes, I've never wanted to be anywhere else."

"You don't think you might want to leave once your grandmother passes on? There are lots of beautiful places on this earth where an artist can be creative. Where people would appreciate your talents."

"No. This is where the clans of my ancestors reside. And my spirit, too. I may not be all that much here in Dinetah, but I would be less than nothing anywhere else."

Teal fell into silence once again. How could she argue with that?

"So you leave us," Lucas's grandmother said with a scowl. "You run away from your destiny."

Teal stopped drying the last of the glasses, put down her dish towel and jammed her hands on her hips. "I am not running away. I've been reassigned. It's my job."

Not nervous anymore, she decided she really liked this old lady with the strange eyes, but it was tough to listen to the scorn in her voice. Lucas had left her here an hour ago. Teal had searched for Snow and found the little black cat curled up asleep in the corner. Some pal.

"You run," Grandmother Helena Gray Goats insisted. "You turn away from the People as you have always turned away from your dreams."

Now the elder was pushing things too far. Teal hadn't wanted to talk about her dreams with Lucas, and she sure as hell wouldn't discuss them with his weird grandmother. She fisted her hands and started toward the bedroom door.

"Sit. The coffee is ready. I have more to tell you."

Teal heaved a heavy sigh and returned to the kitchen table. She was suddenly exhausted. But not like when the old lady had slipped her a sleeping potion. No. This tired feeling was more in her soul than in her body.

Grandmother Gray Goats poured two mugs of coffee and sat down beside her. The old woman's voice was low as she stared into the cup before her.

She told Teal the Dineh creation story. "After they were created, First Man and First Woman had five sets of twins. Then they had an argument and parted, each taking the children of their own sex. After a few years apart, the people realized that male and female do need each other.

"Changing Woman was one of their children," Grandmother continued. "She married the Sun and went west to live with him. On her way, Changing Woman instructed the people in the ways of *hozho,* harmony. That one man needs one woman to find balance."

Finally, she gazed over to Teal and pinned her with those odd, one-black-one-blue eyes. "You are the one for my grandson. You are his destiny."

"No." Teal denied it vehemently. "I've ruined his life. It's better if I go."

"But you are also destined to help the Dineh. To be the stargazer in my place."

"Me? Why would you say that?"

"Look at the signs, Daughter. You can talk to the Bird People and have seen the future in your dreams. You're…"

Teal shot straight up and waved her hands, trying to stop the old woman's words.

But Grandmother ignored her and kept right on

talking. "You saw your father's death weeks before it happened, did you not?"

Sinking low in her chair, Teal bit her lip. Yes, she had dreamed of her father's drowning. Had clearly seen it about to happen. Yet she had done nothing to change the outcome, nothing to save his life. She'd wanted to fish, to be out on the water with him on a bright blue summer day.

After that, after he was buried, was when she had first refused to acknowledge her dreams. Never again. The pain of being so selfish and so...alive when he was dead still pricked at her subconscious mind.

"You were a child," Grandmother said in a soothing voice. "There was nothing you could've done to change what was meant to be. That takes age, wisdom.

"But you have also seen my grandson in your dreams. You knew you would love him before you met. Isn't that true?"

"This isn't love," Teal cried. "It's hell."

She had screamed out the words, knowing full well the old woman had no concept of what hell might be. Teal had already learned that traditional Navajos believed death was just what it looked like. A release of your wind spirit forever. Once the evil spirits of *chindi* disappeared from the body, then the person was gone from this life.

That didn't seem so outrageous a concept any more. But Teal refused to hear another word from Lucas's grandmother about her destiny. It was all bull. Her *destiny* was to be an FBI agent in Durango, Colorado. Or wherever else the Bureau sent her. She wasn't meant to stay here, gazing off into a hazy dreamworld and ruining her lover's life.

She stood up and raced into the bathroom, determined not to think about any of it. Not about the dreams. Not about her destiny.

And sure as hell, not about the man she loved whose life would never ever be the same again.

# Chapter 15

Teal crept through Lucas's front door with Snow hugged tightly to her chest. They'd agreed to leave before dawn and Lucas was to pick her up at his grandmother's so they could get on the road early. But he was late.

Snow made a low growling sound and began to struggle for freedom. Teal shushed him and flipped on a light. The harsh glare illuminated a house turned upside down.

The sofa was tipped on its side, the books were off the shelves. What on earth had happened here? And where was Lucas?

A creepy feeling zinged up her spine and the hairs stood up on the back of her neck. Had the Skinwalkers come for him?

She automatically reached for her weapon, only to remember that it was packed away in her suitcase in Lucas's SUV. Great.

Dropping Snow to the floor, she watched the cat slink away into the darkness. He looked as if he was on the prowl. Hunting for intruders, perhaps.

Teal took a quick look around. Was this the work of burglars? Or a kidnapping?

She stopped, listening for any sound. No sounds except for the ticking of a clock, unseen off in the kitchen. But the scent of Lucas was strong here. It was strong in her dreams, too. Would she ever really be free of the smell of him?

As she searched for some clue as to what had happened, Teal realized what she had been seeing. The walls and pedestals were bare. Someone had come in and stolen all of Lucas's artwork.

Oh, God. Had he caught them at it and tried to stop the thieves? He was an artist, for heaven's sake, not a cop. Why hadn't he called for her help?

In a growing panic about his welfare, she made her way through the darkness. Stepping as quietly as possible through the jumble of furniture on the floor, Teal checked the bedrooms and kitchen. No sign of Lucas anywhere. And no real sign of a struggle. No blood.

As she entered his studio, she heard a distant bass voice, seeming to come from outside the floor-to-ceiling windows. Somewhere nearby, a man was chanting in Navajo, and the voice was being carried by a wailing wind.

Her whole body began to shake with terror. Where was Lucas?

* * *

Lucas squatted down on his heels and hung his head. It was done. Things would be better now for Teal. He was positive.

"*Oh, Lucas*. You're here. Are you all right? What's been going on?"

He'd taken too long. Damn. He hadn't wanted her to know about this. Hadn't wanted her to see…

"Answer me, please. Are you injured?"

He felt as though he'd run two Iron Man competitions in one morning, and he knew he looked worse than that. Shaking and dripping with sweat, he refused to look up at her.

"Everything is fine, Bright Eyes. No problem."

"I was worried. You were late coming for me and I walked over to see why, and I found…"

"I'm sorry I worried you," he interrupted. "And I wish you'd waited for me. It's dangerous to be out walking at this time of night."

Out of the corner of his eye, he saw her bend to pick up a frame. A broken frame that he'd pitched atop the stack of others.

Coming up to his full height, his knees almost gave out on him. He felt that he was falling apart. But the worst was over. All that was left now was to drive her away from the danger.

She turned, with the distorted frame in her hand and a horrified expression on her face. "What's been going on out here? Who did this?"

"It's nothing. Are you ready to go?"

"Go? Not until you explain. I want to know what's happened to thousands of dollars worth of your artwork."

Standing there and glaring at him as the first rays of dawn swept over the cliff behind him, she was definitely the most beautiful woman that had ever lived. If he was still any kind of artist, he would paint that image. It was the face he never wanted to forget.

How could he have taken so much from her? She'd offered him the warmth of her smile, the boundless energy of her company—her entire life force. She had nearly died due to his mistake, and yet she'd stuck with him through everything.

And now her career was pretty much ruined, too. He didn't know a lot about the FBI's method of promotion, but he was positive she was going to be out of the loop for a long while.

The destruction he'd taken all night to accomplish might be of some help. But Teal was going to have to work harder and smarter to overcome her career setback.

"I said it's nothing, Bright Eyes. The decision to destroy the sand paintings was a long time coming. I never should've painted them in the first place."

"You did this? Ripped apart the frames and scattered the colored sand around the yard. All that work, gone?"

He wanted to take her hand, wanted desperately to hold her close. One more time.

But he couldn't. One whisper of her body any closer

than five feet from his and he'd be done for. A puddle of useless emotion.

Instead he sighed and tried to soothe her. "In Navajo mythology, witchcraft is a metaphor for anyone who goes against the Way. Anyone who chooses riches over balance. Anyone who lets greed tip them off the scales of harmony.

"I was a shaman. A healer for the People. I should've known better than to make and sell sand paintings. It's okay for those artists who aren't Singers and don't also make sacred drawings. But I knew the right way and ignored it. I broke the taboos.

"For forgetting them, I deserved to be punished. But I'm sorry for all the trouble I've caused you."

"Oh, Lucas." She reached out and took a step in his direction.

He backed up, keeping the distance he needed. Teal would forgive him anything, he knew. The girl in his dreams loved him and if he asked, he knew she would stay.

But he wouldn't ask.

"Lucas, let me help you. Maybe together…"

"No, Bright Eyes. I'd give my life to be the guy you needed. That fellow who's been appearing in your dreams. But that's not the real me.

"For you I'd try to change," he went on. "But you're the strong one. Now be strong enough to do what's best for both of us."

Right then, Snow appeared at the open studio door. He captured everyone's attention in an instant with a sorrowful but loud meow.

Both humans turned to him. Lucas chuckled, then realized what the cat must want.

"Take Snow with you, Bright Eyes."

"With me? To Durango, you mean? I couldn't."

"Yes, you can. He loves you and wants to go. He'll be miserable here without you. Don't you hear him begging?"

"But Lucas, he's your friend. You'll be losing your companion."

"You need a friend in your new place more than I do here. Take him and I won't worry so much about you being all alone."

He stepped over and picked up the black lump of fur with one swipe. "I think his old carrying case is still around here somewhere. Take him, while I go find it." He plopped the cat into her arms and turned away.

From behind his back, he heard her whispering to Snow. Then heard the words he knew would be seared into his consciousness for all eternity.

"Oh, Lucas. I'm so sorry."

They'd left the Mustang Gas, Convenience and Deli store at Teec Nos Pos behind ten minutes ago. Teal was already out of coffee and trying not to think about facing her new life without Lucas.

Why was she leaving a man she'd only now decided she loved? Yes, she remembered she had a job. But wasn't finding some compromise with Lucas every bit as important as the FBI?

He needed her. And come to think of it, she needed him, too. She didn't want to be just one of the guys anymore. He was the first person who'd ever made her really feel like a woman.

And besides that, she had to admit living with him on the reservation would never be boring.

Looking out over the buff-colored sand and rock toward the shimmering pale blue of Ute Mountain in the distance, Teal was finding it hard to stay still. Was it only leaving Lucas that was bothering her? It seemed like that should be enough to ruin her day, since it was probably going to ruin her entire life.

But something else was nagging at her subconscious. She couldn't put her finger on what. Somehow, her cop's instincts were acting up. How odd.

She turned to check on Snow in his carrier in the second seat. The cat was quiet but not asleep. His ears were perked up, his eyes wide and unblinking.

Shooting a quick glance at Lucas in the driver's seat, her heart sank once again. How would she ever be able to go on with a life that didn't include him?

"Why aren't we driving to Durango through Shiprock and Farmington?" she asked, instead of saying all the words that were at the tip of her tongue. "Why go this back route?"

"I want to get you north of the San Juan River as fast as possible. Off the reservation. It'll be safer if we go through Cortez."

"You believe the Skinwalkers would hunt us down in your SUV?"

"They know you know about them, Teal. And you could make trouble for them, too—maybe in Washington. I don't think they'll be happy to have you outside their influence.

"Here in Dinetah, the Skinwalkers have the People cowered," he continued. "Too afraid to say anything about them. The evil ones can't be thrilled about an FBI agent who knows of their existence and is getting away."

"Oh, well..."

Another couple of cars sped past them going west, back toward Teec Nos Pos. At that very moment, the highway curved around a huge boulder. Up ahead she could see the bridge at Four-Corners that would lead them away from the Navajo reservation and Arizona and into the Ute reservation and Colorado.

A chill lifted the hairs on the back of Teal's neck. A gray cloud moved overhead and blocked out the morning sunshine.

Teal opened her mouth to say she didn't like the way things were beginning to feel. But just then a scrawny-looking dog darted out from behind the boulder and ran into the road. The animal made it as far as the opposite lane a few yards in front of them. Then it stopped, turned and stared directly at their oncoming SUV.

She heard Lucas mumble something about a coyote under his breath, then felt him press down hard on the brakes. By the time she looked straight ahead again, an old Navajo woman carrying a child had stepped out into the road directly in front of them.

The next few seconds were a blur of motion. Lucas swerved the SUV slightly, but there was no place to go. To the left the coyote still stood in place on the road. Straight ahead was a disaster waiting to happen.

Teal screamed and automatically reached over to help him pull against the wheel, trying to force the SUV to make a sudden change in direction. Lucas was yelling something about Skinwalkers as he jammed the brakes. To their right was the huge boulder.

Dragging the wheel to the right anyway, she hoped like hell their vehicle would miss both the boulder — and the old lady and the kid.

It did. But with a cloud of dust and a rumble of tires against gravel, the SUV left the road still moving too fast.

Her heart jumped into her throat as they careened down a steep embankment. She threw Lucas a quick look and saw him desperately standing on the brakes, fruitlessly working to stop the SUV's forward motion.

With a gasp, a whoosh and a sickening thud, the SUV hit the water, landing right-side-up in the San Juan River.

And sinking fast.

A strange, misplaced notion had Teal thinking how lucky they'd been to land in a spot with deeper water. Downstream, sandy island tops stuck up out of the water's flow, blocking the river and causing little eddies toward each bank. Landing on one of those islands off the steep cliff from the road would've probably killed them instantly.

To flash her into the moment, the SUV's front seat filled with water almost immediately. She didn't have time for any other thoughts. Icy fingers of river water lapped at her chest.

Reaching for her seat belt, Teal fumbled with the catch. Oh, God. Now was no time for her to be klutzy.

Her fingers were so cold after fifteen seconds in the water that they were already numb. She could barely move.

"Let me," Lucas yelled as he reached over with his hunting knife and slit the seat belt in two.

She was free. But now she had to figure out a way to get out of the SUV. Fast.

Through the rising water, she felt Lucas grab her arm. "Keep back and watch your eyes," he hollered, his mouth only inches above the top of the water.

Teal blinked and heard a cracking noise. When she looked up, Lucas had managed to reach over her and crack the glass of the passenger-side window with some kind of sharp tool. Then he was shoving hard at big unbroken glass pieces, still hanging by a thread.

"Go," he urged as he pushed one last time.

The force he used did the trick, but instantly the front seat filled—over her head and closing in. It covered her with muddy, cold water.

A blinding pain in her temples from the icy water seared straight through to her mind. A flare of memory from the last time she'd been over her head in water by surprise spurred her out the window and to the surface of the river.

Gasping for breath, Teal swam for the nearest bank.

Thank heaven she'd learned to swim since the last
time she'd nearly drowned at age eleven.

She reached the shore and put her feet down into the
mud, sinking up to her ankles. A small crowd had
gathered on the bank and a man reached his hand out to
help her.

"Is there anyone else in there?" he yelled.

Teal turned her head back to see the top of the SUV
sinking fast beneath the water. *There was no sign of
Lucas!* And none of Snow, either!

Where was Lucas? And how could she have fled the
scene without remembering to save poor Snow, who'd
been locked in his traveling cage?

Omigod. She'd saved herself and never given a
thought to…

This nightmare could not be a repeat of her father's
death. She would not allow it to happen. It would
surely kill her this time.

She let go of the bystander's hand and pulled
herself free of the mud by diving back into the water.
Half the way back to the SUV she saw Snow's head
breaking the ripples as he began swimming toward
her. His little paws were treading water like mad.
Lucas must have gotten him out of his carrying case.
Thank heaven!

Reaching him in an instant, she grabbed the cat by
the scruff of the neck and gave him a huge shove
toward the shore. That should get him close enough for
the bystanders to reach.

Then she turned around to find Lucas. *Oh, please,
don't let him die.* He must've stayed to rescue Snow.

Teal's chest swelled, more from pride in the man than with the air she was taking in order to dive back under the water. Lucas had sacrificed himself for her safety—and for the cat she loved.

It was just like him to do that. It had been just like that for her father, too.

No-o-o.

She ducked under, but found she couldn't see anything in the murky water. Lifting her head, she checked the river one more time. Where was he?

Back under she went, determined to find him. She fumbled to the SUV's side without being able to see and realized Lucas's inert body was stuck half-in and half-out of the passenger window. She felt around and found where his shirt was caught on a broken piece of glass.

With a scream lodged in her throat and her lungs desperate for air, Teal vowed her nightmare would not end this way again. She ripped at the glass and cut her hands in the process. But it didn't matter. The damned glass would not stop her. Nothing would.

Then in the next instant, Lucas's body was free—and now was rapidly sinking deadweight. Refusing to consider the implications of that, she took him in the lifesaving headlock she'd learned back at a Quantico pool. And she swam for his life.

"Lucas?" Teal's voice sounded rough, gravelly as it faded in and out of his conscious mind.

Raising a hand, he felt the warmth and silkiness of her cheek under his fingers. "Bright Eyes."

He was sure he'd been dreaming. But when he blinked open his lids, she was there.

Remembering now that she'd pulled him out of the water and had brought him around using CPR, he tried to find a memory of what had happened to him since then. It was hazy, and all he really recalled was being sheltered in the refuge of her arms as an ambulance's wail seemed to signal they were racing through the Dinetah countryside.

"Shush," she whispered. "Don't try to talk. You're in the Farmington hospital, and you're going to be fine. The doctors say you only have to stay overnight. Then you can go home."

There was a strange twinge in her voice that worried him. Was she trying to say goodbye again? By tomorrow she would have to be in Durango. He remembered that much.

He wasn't sure he could stand it, losing her now. Seeing her walk away. Not since she'd saved his life. Not since he'd discovered how his life would be worthless without her.

At that very moment when he'd pushed her through the broken SUV window and watched her swim toward the surface, he'd known for sure. And for that moment, he had believed.

The two of them were meant to be. In dreams, in life, or even in death.

Now he lay still and silent—and wondered, trying not to succumb to too much despair. Was this the end? He tried to focus.

Her face came into view through a watery film that clouded his eyes. "Don't go, Teal."

"I'm not going anywhere."

"I don't mean…" A cough interrupted his words and he swallowed hard against the emotion that seemed to be clogging his throat.

He was ready to beg. To plead with her if necessary. They had to have their chance. The opportunity to change their destiny.

"Hush," she said on a soft sigh. "Don't say anything. I have something to say to you anyway.

"I almost lost you." She hurried the words out. "It made me realize I'd been wrong. Wrong to think I could ever be happy apart from you.

"I can't, Lucas. I can't ever leave you. I know you thought you were doing me a big favor, protecting me from Skinwalkers. But how can you protect me if I'm miles away?"

She stopped, sniffed once, then raced ahead. "I'm not going anywhere. Not ever. I've resigned from the Bureau. Neither you, the FBI nor the Skinwalkers can make me leave the rez. If you won't let me stay with you, then I'll live with your grandmother. Right down the road. I'll drive you crazy pestering…"

He reached up, placed a finger against her lips and let his hopes soar. "It's okay, my love. I've realized I can't live without you, either. I don't want to be the lonely guy nobody pays attention to anymore. I want to share my dreams, my whole waking life—with you.

"Marry me. Love me." His voice faltered, became

a whisper that hurt his throat. "Without you, I don't make sense. Please, love me."

Tears rolled down her cheeks, surprising him. "Oh, Lucas. I've loved you for forever. Of course I'll marry you. Just try to stop me."

As the last rays of a spectacular autumn sun turned the Four-Corners skies to a splashy magenta, two people melded their lives together. Black and white mixed to become not quite gray, but a breathtaking shade of silver.

The same color as in the traditional silver bands the groom would make for the two of them to wear on the third fingers of their left hands—the same bands that would be leading them to all their dreams and tomorrows.

# *Epilogue*

Brand-new Navajo Tribal Police Investigator Teal Benaly Tso, watched as her husband's cousin, Michael Ayze, laid out his equipment on the floor of Lucas's medicine hogan. As her medicine man for this Blessingway Sing, Michael had already shown her exactly where to sit for the curing ceremony. He was now taking things from the medicine bundle he'd been wearing earlier.

For weeks, Teal had been studying and learning, getting her traditional training from Grandmother Gray Goats. Feeling only slightly silly now at being the object of this intense scrutiny from her new clansmen, Teal thought about the solemn way Michael lifted out his prayersticks, bags of pollen and arrow flints, laying them on the ground before him. There would be sand paintings drawn and destroyed here over the next two days. She would be required to walk on some of them as chants would be sung.

Outside, all her new family, including her new husband, were waiting to help her celebrate this ceremony done to bring her back into harmony with her spirit. She'd imagined this Sing would not mean that much to her, since she was so totally happy and in balance with her brand-new life anyway. But to keep harmony in her family, she'd agreed.

Lucas had been the one who'd really needed an extended ceremony. He'd had his done before the two of them got married. Now her husband was finding new ways to be creative and had just finished an oil painting—of crimson rain falling through a golden Navajo sunset.

He was also back to being a Brotherhood warrior. The one who could communicate with the Bird People, along with his wife. His whole life had changed, and she was proud to be a big part of the reason he smiled all the time now.

Two days later, after a long night of chanting, Teal obeyed orders and took in the right number of ceremonial breaths as the healing spirit took over her body. She felt different. Calmer. Walking in beauty.

But, deep inside, her hidden spirit also kept its determined cop's instincts. Sometime during her ceremony, Teal had finally realized that the vision of the woman and the baby on the bridge before their accident had been nothing but a magic trick done by Skinwalkers. But the Brotherhood had not yet located the Skin-walker Burrowing Owl or the Navajo Wolf. And she would be damned if she would rest until they did. Of course, now when she found them, she wouldn't want to punish them. No, only to take away their evil with the proper ceremony and to bring them back into their own harmony.

Not so bothered by the differences between black and white anymore, Teal ignored the contrary thoughts of witches for the moment and couldn't wait to be back at the side of her husband. The man who'd brought her more than love. The man who'd given her the twin silver circles of clan and harmony.

And for that, he was destined to forever be her dream lover.

\* \* \* \* \*

*Turn the page for a sneak preview of*
*IF I'D NEVER KNOWN YOUR LOVE*
*by*
*Georgia Bockoven*

*From the brand-new series*
*Harlequin Everlasting Love*
*Every great love has a story to tell.*™

*One year, five months and four days missing*

There's no way for you to know this, Evan, but I haven't written to you for a few months. Actually, it's been almost a year. I had a hard time picking up a pen once more after we paid the second ransom and then received a letter saying it wasn't enough. I was so sure you were coming home that I took the kids along to Bogotá so they could fly home with you and me, something I swore I'd never do. I've fallen in love with Colombia and the people who've opened their hearts to me. But fear is a constant companion when I'm there. I won't ever expose our children to that kind of danger again.

I'm at a loss over what to do anymore, Evan. I've begged and pleaded and thrown temper tantrums with every official I can corner both here and at home. They've been incredibly tolerant and understanding, but in the end as ineffectual as the rest of us.

I try to imagine what your life is like now, what you do every day, what you're wearing, what you eat. I want to believe that the people who have you are misguided yet kind, that they treat you well. It's how I survive day to day. To think of you being mistreated hurts too much. If I picture you locked away somewhere and suffering, a weight descends on me that makes it almost impossible to get out of bed in the morning.

Your captors surely know you by now. They have to recognize what a good man you are. I imagine you working with their children, telling them that you have children, too, showing them the pictures you carry in your wallet. Can't the men who have you understand how much your children miss you? How can it not matter to them?

How can they keep you away from us all this time? Over and over, we've done what they asked. Are they oblivious to the depth of their cruelty? What kind of people are they that they don't care?

I used to keep a calendar beside our bed next to the peach rose you picked for me before you left. Every night I marked another day, counting how many you'd been gone. I don't do that any longer. I don't want to be reminded of all the days we'll never get back.

When I can't sleep at night, I tell you about my day. I imagine you hearing me and smiling over the details that make up my life now. I never tell you how defeated I feel at moments or how hard I work to hide it from everyone for fear they will see it as a reason to stop believing you are coming home to us.

And I couldn't tell you about the lump I found in my breast and how difficult it was going through all the tests without you here to lean on. The lump was benign—the process reaching that diagnosis utterly terrifying. I couldn't stop thinking about what would happen to Shelly and Jason if something happened to me.

We need you to come home.

I'm worn down with missing you.

I'm going to read this tomorrow and will probably tear it up or burn it in the fireplace. I don't want you to get the idea I ever doubted what I was doing to free you or thought the work a burden. I would gladly spend the rest of my life at it, even if, in the end, we only had one day together.

You are my life, Evan.

I will love you forever.

\* \* \* \* \*

*Don't miss this deeply moving
Harlequin Everlasting Love story about a woman's
struggle to bring back her kidnapped husband from
Colombia and her turmoil over whether to let go,
finally, and welcome another man into her life.
IF I'D NEVER KNOWN YOUR LOVE
by Georgia Bockoven
is available March 27, 2007.*

*And also look for
THE NIGHT WE MET
by Tara Taylor Quinn,
a story about finding love
when you least expect it.*

# HARLEQUIN Romance®

presents a brand-new trilogy by

# PATRICIA THAYER

*Rocky Mountain*
# BRIDES

**Three sisters come home to wed.**

*In April don't miss*

# Raising the Rancher's Family,

*followed by*

# The Sheriff's Pregnant Wife,

on sale May 2007,

**and**

# A Mother for the Tycoon's Child,

on sale June 2007.

# nocturne™

## IT'S TIME TO DISCOVER THE RAINTREE TRILOGY...

**There have always been those among us who are more than human...**

**Don't miss the dramatic first book by**
*New York Times* **bestselling author**

# LINDA HOWARD

## Raintree: *Inferno*

**On sale May.**

*Raintree: Haunted* by Linda Winstead Jones
**Available June.**

*Raintree: Sanctuary* by Beverly Barton
**Available July.**

# REQUEST YOUR FREE BOOKS!

## 2 FREE NOVELS PLUS 2 FREE GIFTS

### Silhouette® Romantic

# SUSPENSE

### Sparked by Danger, Fueled by Passion!

## Silhouette Desire

**Introducing talented new author**

# TESSA RADLEY

*making her Silhouette Desire debut
this April with*

## BLACK WIDOW BRIDE

**Book #1794
Available in April 2007.**

Wealthy Damon Asteriades had no choice but to
force Rebecca Grainger back to his family's estate—
despite his vow to keep away from her seductive
charms. But being so close to the woman society once
dubbed the Black Widow Bride had him aching to
claim her as his own...at any cost.

### On sale April from Silhouette Desire!

**Available wherever books are sold,
including most bookstores, supermarkets,
discount stores and drugstores.**

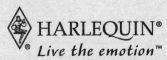

Silhouette®
Romantic
## SUSPENSE

# COMING NEXT MONTH

### #1459 DESI'S RESCUE—Ruth Wind

*Sisters of the Mountain*

Desi Rousseau was a suspect in her estranged husband's murder, and with the police willing to stop there, she resolved to get the answers herself. She wasn't prepared when hard as nails Tamati Neville offered to help clear her name, but she was desperate enough to take help wherever it was offered—and the fact that he was every woman's fantasy didn't hurt.

### #1460 DIAGNOSIS: DANGER—Marie Ferrarella

*The Doctors Pulaski*

A pediatrician attracts the attention of an off-duty detective when she refuses to back down about her friend's death. Together they try to solve the mystery of his murder and discover that love can bloom in the strangest places.

### #1461 THE PERFECT STRANGER—Jenna Mills

Detective John D'Ambrosia can't believe the woman he shared an incredible night with weeks ago is investigating the same case. Saura convinces him that he needs her to capture the villain, and against his better judgment he agrees. But can he survive his desire for his partner?

### #1462 WARRIOR FOR ONE NIGHT—Nancy Gideon

When an undercover investigation leads Detective Xander Caufield to a charter security service, he isn't prepared for the onslaught of attraction for the woman assigned to "guard" him. Now he must battle his growing feelings for his protector...and potential suspect.